THE DEVIOUS KIND

CLINT WESTGARD

ALSO BY CLINT WESTGARD

Mystery/Crime/Thrillers:

All Down the Line (short story)

Stand By Your Man (short story)

The Adventures of Holly Amos: A Western (forthcoming)

Fantasy and Science Fiction:

The Maleficio Chronicles

The Shadow Men:

    Realm of Shadows

    Council of Shadows

    Dance of Shadows

The Sojourners Cycle:

    The Forgotten

    The Apostate

    The Acolyte (forthcoming)

The Trials of the Minotaur

Published by Lost Quarter Books
www.lostquarterbooks.com

For Angelica, for everything.

1

The body lay, sprawled awkwardly, partway down the coulee, right before the slope turned sheer and plunged to the creek far below. The night had hidden it, but the arrival of dawn made its presence obvious. There were several sets of footprints from where the body lay to the road, clearly marked in the muddy spring ground. Even as the new day's light revealed these details, the first flakes of snow began to fall, wet and heavy. For a time the earth resisted their intrusion, but eventually the storm proved too much and the ground turned white, covering over the tracks.

Wayne Johnstone noticed the body later that morning. By then the snow had covered all but the person's red jacket, which stood out vividly against the backdrop of white snow and the drab browns and greys of late March on the Canadian prairies. There was no green yet anywhere, not even any buds on the trees, spring only tentatively taking hold. The arrival of the storm promised that winter would not yet go quietly.

Even still he almost missed it, distracted by his worry about the storm's arrival. He had one hundred fifty cows still to calve and they were coming in bunches now. If the storm was as big as promised—and it looked to be, the snow descending so thickly he sometimes had trouble making out the highway—then he would likely lose some calves today.

There was little he could do about it, but it still worked at his thoughts, as he drove the tractor into the far pen where he turned out the cows who had already calved. Many were already tucked into the slat-fenced shelter near the gate, but they followed him deeper into the pen, heads low against the snow, waiting for the feed to emerge from the tub grinder.

It was as he reached the end of the first row of feed, and turned the tractor around to start the second, that he caught sight of the red jacket. Thinking it was something that had come off a passing car, he drove to the edge of the pen by the lip of the slope to see what it might be. Something in him recognized just what and who it was immediately, and he sat in the tractor, his hands clutching the steering wheel, feeling very cold.

After a time he clambered down the hillside, now slick with the accumulating snow, to confirm his suspicions. He stood looking down at her, the snow gathering on his shoulders and hat, before he managed to gather himself and return to the tractor. He reached into his pocket for his cell phone to call Diane, but stopped himself. Somehow it didn't seem right announcing this to her over the phone. He got back into the tractor and finished up with the last row for the cattle, before returning to the house.

He left the tractor running and went inside. Diane was in the kitchen lingering over her last cup of coffee. He called her from the entryway and she ducked her head around the corner to look at him, a frown on her face, knowing there had to be something wrong for him to have come in so soon after leaving.

"I just found Kristi Taid's body in the coulee," he said after a moment's hesitation. Saying the words made it feel much more real.

Diane seemed to not understand. "What's she doing out there?"

"She's dead," Wayne said with a heavy sigh. "Shotgun to the head."

"Oh," Diane said, reflecting and staring off glassy-eyed into the distance. "Better call the police, I guess."

Wayne was already fishing into his pocket to remove his cell phone. "Do you have the number?"

"Well, just 911, right? This has to be an emergency. My God, poor Leonard. I wonder if Clarissa's home."

Wayne nodded, realizing he had never in his life called the emergency line before. He stared at the flip phone in his hands, pulling it open gingerly, still unsure of the device. Diane had insisted he get one in case of emergencies, but the phone did not feel comfortable in his hands. Using it was still not intuitive. Briefly, he found himself wondering if he needed to dial a different emergency number for cell phones only, before dismissing that as ridiculous. Now he dialed and waited, listening to the ring.

"I'm going to call Leonard," Diane said.

"Don't," Wayne said, as the operator began to speak. "The police won't like that."

"I have to," Diane said.

Wayne knew better than to argue. He talked with the operator, telling what he had seen, and was told the constable would be on his way shortly. The detachment was in Loverna, Wayne knew, half an hour away. Probably more in the snow. He had time enough to get a few of the chores done before this new storm descended upon him, and he headed out the door to do so.

2

Half an hour later, a police car drove slowly up the driveway into the main yard, pulling to a stop in front of the ranch house, where Diane stood on the porch, a dog at her feet and a hood thrown over her head to keep off the snow.

"Hello, Diane," Constable Martin Tomas said as he stepped out of the car.

She just nodded. "It's down there by the coulee," she said, pointing. "You can take your car if you think it can make it through the mud."

"I'll be all right."

She paused, and then said, "We called him. Wayne said I probably shouldn't, but I had to."

He nodded. "He's down there now?"

"Yeah."

Martin got back into his car and drove slowly down the laneway that led to the far pens that edged onto the coulee. He went past pens filled with cattle still heavy with their winter coats, but he paid them no mind. Even six months ago he might have, but now, a year and a half into his term here, a cow was just a cow.

He arrived at the gate to the far corral, and could see

Wayne's truck, a brand new 2003 Dodge Ram, parked by the fence and, on the other side, two figures staring down at the ground. Martin knew what they were looking at. He debated driving his car through the pen, but decided it was a poor idea. The ground would be soft in there, and the last thing he needed on a day like this was to get stuck in a corral.

It would have been easier, he realized, peering through the snow, if he had gone out to the highway and parked there, coming down through the ditch to the coulee. That was likely what had happened with whoever had killed Kristi Taid. With that thought, he reversed course and went out to the highway, parking his car on the shoulder and putting his hazards on, hoping that anyone who happened down the road would be able to see enough to spot them.

He stepped and slid his way from the road down into the ditch and from there made his way gingerly down the incline toward the coulee. A fence ran along the highway, ending at the coulee's edge, and Martin found himself wondering why Wayne hadn't bothered to extend it further. The coulee was part of his land and there was a pasture down below, but likely there was a fence somewhere there to keep the cattle from it.

Not that the cattle would be likely to ever make there way from the ravine's bottom up the highway. Even from its edge, Martin could not make out the coulee's bottom, could not see the creek that twisted and wound its way through its narrow passes. Trees, short and narrow-trunked, like all prairie trees, lined either side, obscuring what lay within.

The two men, both with lean rancher's frames made bulky by the winter clothes they were wearing, were watching as he approached. Martin could not make out their expressions through the swirl of the snow falling, for which he was oddly glad. He set his shoulders and nodded at them.

"Hello, Martin. Thanks for coming," Wayne said. He was a tall man, and would have been gangly in his youth. Age had thickened him somewhat and now, in his early sixties, he appeared as a solid presence beside the more sleight Leonard, still powerful, in spite of his age.

"No problem," Martin said, an automatic reply, which sounded stupid, given the situation.

The other man, hood up on his jacket, hunched over to better keep his face clear of snow, did not say anything. His eyes had not strayed from the ground where the body lay. Martin looked at him carefully, now that he was up close, but his expression was blank. He seemed not to even realize that someone else had arrived on the scene. Well, it was his wife on the ground, after all.

Wayne moved aside so that Martin could get near the body. Martin stepped in, smiling his thanks and crouched over the body. The face was mostly blown away. He could see the outline of one eye socket and most of the jaw, bits of brain and skull. Her neck and chest were perforated with pellet blasts. The blood was that curdled dark color, clumping against her skin and the earth below. He sighed and stood up, turning to Leonard.

"It's her, all right," Leonard said. "That's her jacket and shoes."

Martin looked at Wayne. "Anybody else been down here but you two?"

Wayne shook his head.

"All right. Why don't you and Leonard head back to the house and wait for me? I want to look around a bit. Cory should be here pretty quick."

"What'll they do with the body?" Leonard asked, his tone odd.

"He'll have to take it into town. Botha will have to look at it. We'll take care of it."

He turned and knelt again by the body. The two others remained where they were, as though unsure of whether they should in fact leave, before Wayne reached out and put an arm on Leonard's shoulder and led him back to the pen. Martin looked up from the body, not leaving his crouch, and watched them get into Wayne's truck and drive back through the corral, the tires leaving clear tracks in the snow.

An eerie quiet descended around him, a product of the stillness that seemed to always come with a snowfall. The only sounds that intruded on his study of the body were the wind cutting through the coulee and the odd cow calling out to a calf in the pen beside him. He could hear his own breathing, which sounded hushed, as if even he did not want to disturb this scene.

It had already been disturbed, though; the snow had seen to that. The body had been dragged here, likely from the highway, given the lack of blood surrounding her and the severity of the gunshot wounds. The snow had already obscured any evidence of that passage, as well as the footprints of whoever had carried her here. There was also the matter of the remainder of her head, which was no doubt in pieces wherever she had been shot.

Where had she been shot and why had she been brought here? He stood up and found himself looking in the direction of the Taid's ranch. It did not make sense that Leonard would bring her here if he wanted to direct attention away from himself, given his home was only a mile away. And if someone else were trying to point the finger in his direction, they would be more likely to make sure her body was found somewhere on his land.

This felt more like an idea that had occurred in passing as the killers rushed to hide the trail that led to them. Dump the body in the coulee and hope the storm, which everyone had known was coming, would hide the body. If they had gotten her farther down into the coulee it very well might have, Martin realized. And if the coyotes had gotten to the body, it might have been a very long time indeed before any trace was found of her.

Which led to another question: why here? Why not take

the body down farther and deeper into the trees? The body lay between two short, shrub-like trees, but without their leaves the body was exposed to both the road and the pen. Whoever had done it was in a rush, working in the dark so that Wayne and Diane didn't chance to see them, perhaps struggling with weight of the corpse. They had come this far and judged it far enough. What had led to that haste, and where had they been going initially before they changed their plans and chose this place to hide the body?

He paced from the body back to the road. The only tracks leading into the ditch were his own, and even they were rapidly disappearing. He climbed back up onto the highway, kicking at the damp blacktop. Soon it too would surrender to the snow, disappearing beneath it. The road curved just ahead along with the coulee, the two running nearly parallel briefly, before it curved again to wrap around the valley. The snow was coming down so heavily he could not see beyond that.

He went back to the body, snapping on the rubber gloves he had brought as he went, feeling faintly ridiculous as he did so. This was his first murder investigation, and he was very conscious of making a misstep and also of being found out for a fraud. That, as much as anything else, had been why he sent Wayne and Leonard away. Though obviously Leonard was very much a suspect, Martin could not have both of them around further contaminating the crime scene.

All he knew about conducting this sort of investigation he had learned at the academy in Regina, though the principles were the same as with any of the dozens of robberies and assaults he had been called in on while here or in Wetaskawin, where he had been stationed previously. It did not feel that way now that he was faced with a dead body. This felt of much greater import. A life had been lost, after all. And it fell to him to determine who had been responsible.

Wiping his eyes clear of water and snow, he knelt down

and gingerly turned what was left of Kristi's head toward him and pulled back her remaining eyelid. The eye beneath was cloudy and the body itself stiff with rigor mortis, no doubt helped by the temperature, which had hovered around the freezing mark for most of the night through to the morning.

Martin stood, clicking his tongue against the roof of his mouth thoughtfully, and started to pull his gloves off when he heard a vehicle approaching. He watched as the ambulance pulled up behind his car and Cory slid his bulk out from behind the wheel. The ambulance driver wandered over, his jeans tucked into unlaced work boots, his jacket open to the elements as well. He was unshaven and, as he came up alongside, Martin caught a whiff of booze.

"Late night?"

"Oh," Cory said with a wave of his hand. His eyes were bloodshot, but that was hardly surprising for Cory. In spite of the fact they were both in their early thirties, Martin always thought of Cory as being much younger. He certainly acted like it.

"You good to drive yet?"

"I made it here, didn't I?"

"Don't make me put the fucking Breathalyzer on you," Martin said. "I've got enough shit to deal with without you cocking things up."

Cory waved his hand again and turned his attention to the body. "Kristi Taid."

"Yes," Martin said.

"Cause of death shouldn't be a problem, anyway."

"No."

"Well, how you wanna do this? Bring the stretcher down from the highway, probably the easiest."

Martin agreed, and they both made their way up the ditch to the back of the ambulance, where they offloaded the stretcher. Together they wheeled it down into the ditch and gingerly set Kristi's body upon it. Beneath where her body had lain was only dormant grass and dead leaves. No doubt he was ruining all kinds of forensic evidence, but who knew how long it would take for the RCMP to send a forensics team out. The storm would only complicate things further, and Martin could not just leave the body here for all the world driving by to see.

Once the body was safely strapped to the stretcher, they wheeled it back up the ditch, both of them slipping and cursing on the slope. When they had the stretcher safely into the back of the ambulance, Cory turned to Martin.

"Take it in to Botha, then?"

"Yes," Martin said. "And for fuck's sake, Cory, don't phone anyone, don't let anyone know. This is an RCMP investigation now."

Cory didn't reply, giving him another wave, and was on his way. Martin sighed and swore again under his breath. He stood and watched until the ambulance had disappeared in the snow. He waited before getting into his own car, looking up at the vast wall of grey clouds above him, already thinking of the questions he would have to ask Leonard.

3

As he turned the car around and headed back to the Johnstone house, he reported the murder to the detachment in Hanna, requesting backup if they had it. The woman in the detachment office told him that all the officers from Youngstown and Hanna were dealing with an accident on Highway 9, but once they were done there they could send someone along. One of them was supposed to be coming anyway, with Lara leaving for the week yesterday, but obviously circumstances had delayed that. She would also put in a request for a forensics team from Calgary to be sent as soon as possible. The way the storm was going, none of them might make it, he thought.

He pulled up in front of the house, stopping behind Leonard's truck, and sat for a moment, unwilling to start this just yet. Why the hell had Lara picked this week for her vacation? The one time when he actually needed the backup, she was visiting her in-laws in BC. He put his hand to his temple as if to stave off a headache, and thought briefly about having a smoke. Lara had told him he should quit, though, and he was trying for her. That thought got him moving again up to the house.

It was the standard sort of ranch house one saw in

these parts, a long single-story with a basement. There was a deck extending off one side that led to a back door and porch, which was where he entered. There was a front door, but Martin knew the only people who used it didn't get let in. The Johnstones' dog raised its head from the mat as he took off his boots, quietly slapping its tail against the floor. There was a row of hooks filled with jackets above the mat, and Martin put his there, taking his hat off as well. Wayne stepped into the porch and gave him a thin smile.

"Come on in, Martin," he said. Martin nodded and noticed that the rubber gloves were still on his hands. He stuffed them in his pockets and followed Wayne down the hall to the kitchen, where Leonard and Diane were waiting for him in awkward silence. He smelled coffee and banana muffins.

"Would you like some coffee, Martin?" Diane asked from where she was busy at the counter. She was a small, bustling presence, with short-cropped dark hair that was speckled with grey she did not bother to hide.

"Please," he said, as he sat opposite Leonard at the kitchen table. Wayne hovered between the counters and the table, unsure where he should put himself.

"Put the muffins out," Diane told him, which he did while she gave Martin his cup of coffee.

He poured a bit of milk in and, while he stirred it, said to them, "I'm going to have to open a formal investigation, obviously, and I'll have to ask you some questions, you understand."

"Of course," Diane said, while the other two nodded.

Martin pulled out his notebook and caught himself for a second imagining Lara's meticulous, careful handwriting. She would be much better suited to these circumstances than he was.

"You checked those cows last night?"

"Yeah," Wayne said, "At ten and just after midnight, and then six. I didn't see anything then, not till this morning, anyway. Don't know that I would've, though."

"You hear anything at all?"

"No—no shots, anyway," Diane said, "We don't hear cars driving by anymore either, just sleep right through it."

Martin raised his cup, blew on the coffee, and took a sip. "Anything else that you can think of? Maybe you saw something unusual yesterday or this morning? Anything could be important."

Both of them shook their heads, and Martin nodded. "All right. I think that's all for the moment. If you could give me a minute with Leonard."

"Sure," Wayne said, looking relieved. "Diane, I could use some help with the chores."

Martin and Leonard both looked at their coffee, listening as Diane and Wayne put on their boots and jackets and went outside. Martin waited until the door had shut. "I'm sorry about this, Leonard. I know this is no time for this, but you understand."

"Of course," Leonard said. He was, Martin guessed, in his early forties, with narrow features, made more so by the absence of hair atop his head. His expression was one of perpetual reserve, that now was tinged with wariness.

"Is Clarissa home yet?"

"Yeah, she is. Came back for the weekend and decided to stay a couple of extra days before she heads back to classes. I haven't even told her."

Martin smiled, hoping it looked reassuring. "I won't keep you long. Kristi wasn't at home last night, then?"

"No, no. She went into town early. And she had a school board meeting at 6:30, I think."

"She didn't come home after?"

"No." Leonard winced as he spoke, his face going a little red.

Martin leaned back in his chair. There had been talk, of course, even he had heard it, about the nature of Leonard and Kristi's relationship. There would be more now. "You know what she was doing?"

"No. No." He paused, and a rueful smile twitched across his lips. "I figured something must have kept her late, and she'd just stayed in with Karen or Carol. She's done that sometimes before."

Martin nodded. Did Leonard genuinely believe that, or was it one of those lies that he had chosen to accept, to make livable a situation that otherwise would not be? The latter, Martin suspected.

"How come she was at the school board meeting?" Martin asked. Clarissa was their only daughter and she had gone to university the year before.

"She decided to stay on for another year after Clarissa left. It's hard to find people to volunteer for these things anymore."

Martin paused, framing the next question in his mind before asking it. "How've things been lately in general? Kristi have any problems with anyone? Any sort of difficulties? That type of thing."

"No. I'm— Everything was normal. I just don't understand."

Normal—an interesting choice of words, Martin thought. "The shop with Carol was doing fine?"

"Oh yeah, yeah. Good as can be expected." Leonard shrugged.

Martin nodded and peered down at his notebook. "You notice anything out of the ordinary yesterday? Was she acting differently at all?"

Leonard sounded tired. "No, it was just—just the way it always was."

"Clarissa was home last night?" Martin glanced up from his notebook, and Leonard gave a single nod. "Nobody else stopped by? Anybody call?"

"I talked to Mike Dzaowoski a bit after supper," Leonard said. "Say, maybe around eight."

"What about?"

"Oh, he had some questions about the REA."

"You're the president, right?"

14

"Not for long if Atco gets its way," Leonard said with a grimace.

"That was it. No one else called?"

Leonard shook his head. Martin drained the rest of his cup and got up to refill it. He held the pot out to Leonard, who waved him away.

"What about Clarissa?" Martin said as he sat back in his chair. "She home all night, or did go somewhere and meet up with some friends?"

"She was home all night. She made supper, actually. And then she was in her room the rest of the night. I think she had some paper she was working on."

Martin set aside his pen. "All right. I think that'll do for now. I'll probably have some more questions when it's a little clearer what happened and when. You better go let Clarissa know. I'm going to have to talk to her too, you understand. I need to confirm your alibi. But I'll give a half-hour to tell her first."

They both stood, and Leonard gripped his hand. "Thanks. Thanks. Catch whoever did this, all right?"

"Of course, of course."

They went outside together into a world turned almost entirely white. The wind picking up swirled the falling snow so that it seemed to swallow everything around them. In the face of the cutting wind, both of them hunched their shoulders and ducked their heads.

Leonard turned to Martin and said, "I'd better call Kevin too, I guess."

Martin was about to tell him not to, that he should be the one to inform Kevin and every other potential suspect, but he realized it was futile. Leonard was not asking for permission; he was telling Martin he was going to do it. People's obligation was to each other out here, not to some constable who had been stationed here the year before and would be gone in five.

"That's fine. I'll have to talk to him today too. I'll be by in about twenty minutes to talk to Clarissa."

As they both went to their vehicles, Diane pulled up in a truck. "You guys done in there?"

"Yeah," Martin said, walking over to her. Leonard went to his truck and drove out to the highway, going very slowly. "Thanks for everything, Diane. Thank Wayne too. If either of you thinks of anything else, give me a call. I'd just ask that none of you talk to anyone about this just yet."

"Anything we can do to help, Martin," Diane said.

He nodded his thanks and got into his car. As he let it warm up, he checked in with dispatch on the status of his backup, and was told that there had been multiple fatalities and that the highway was shut down. *Of all the days for this*, he thought.

They'd be lucky to make it here by tomorrow, especially if the storm lasted all day. For all intents and purposes, then, he was on his own.

4

Martin first returned to the coulee's edge, where the body had been discovered. In the time he had spent talking to Leonard and Wayne and Diane, all their footprints had nearly been obscured. There was already two inches on snow on the ground, and it was even starting to stick on the blacktop. He was going to have a hell of a time getting back into town, he realized. Hopefully Cory made it back without incident, although that was wishful thinking. There was always an incident with Cory, and he just had to plan around it.

He walked up and down the ditch, about fifteen feet on either side of where the body had been found, kicking at the snow and tall grass to see if anything had been left behind along with the body. Next he turned his attention to the area immediately surrounding where the body had been. Already the snow covered over the ground, and Martin estimated in an hour or so the impression left by Kristi's body would be gone.

Remembering the forensics team, Martin ran back to his car and got some caution pylons from his trunk, swearing at himself that he hadn't thought to bring something more useful, and set them out at the head and feet of the body's impression. He did not bother with the emergency tape, reasoning that nobody but Wayne or Leonard would have any need to come by here, and they would each have sense enough not to. For anyone else passing by, the tape would only serve as an invitation to look closer, and he wanted to avoid having anyone trampling over the ground more than it already had.

That done, Martin searched the area around the body, going in a radius of about fifteen feet and finding nothing. He stopped and looked around, blinking at the snow, which was so thick now it almost rendered his car and the highway invisible. Had he missed anything?

It felt like he must have, but he could think of nothing more. Glancing at his watch, he saw that he still had ten minutes before the half-hour he had promised Leonard was up, and so he went over the whole area again just to be absolutely certain he had not missed anything.

When he was finished, he drove the half-mile to the Taid ranch. It was slow going, the visibility reduced to almost nothing. He pulled into the long driveway and parked in front of the house beside what he assumed was Clarissa's car. Leonard was there to greet him at the door, his eyes red and puffy.

"She's upstairs," he said as Martin stepped out of the snow. "Do you want me to bring her down?"

"I'll go upstairs, if you don't mind," Martin said. "I won't be long."

Leonard nodded distractedly. "First door on the left. Hell of a storm. I'm going to have to plow the driveway or we won't be able to get out."

Martin smiled but did not reply, and went upstairs. Clarissa was nineteen, Kristi and Leonard's only daughter. She had been off at university since Martin's arrival at the detachment and he could count on one hand the number of times they had met. Her cheeks were still wet when she opened the door, and she looked at Martin with a mixture of anger and desperation.

"I'm sorry, Clarissa," he said in a formal voice. "This is not the time for this, but I do have to ask you some questions. It could help me find whoever did this to your mother."

Clarissa gave an abortive half-nod and pointed at her room. "Do you want to do it here?"

"Sure. This won't take long, I promise," and he gestured for her to go in. She sat on the edge of the bed and Martin pulled out a chair wedged under a desk. Now that he was here, he regretted coming in. It felt too personal. But he wanted to get her away from her father, to make sure he could eliminate him as a suspect.

"When did you come home, Clarissa?" he said.

"Friday. After classes." She spoke in a monotone, not meeting his eyes.

"So you spent the weekend here with your mom and dad. Everything seemed normal with her, with them?"

"Yeah, yeah. Everything was just like it always was, you know."

"Okay," he said. "Is there anyone you can think of who had a disagreement with your mom that you know about? Did she tell you about any arguments that she had?"

"Mom had lots of *disagreements*. Everybody does here. It's what people live on, that and the gossip. But nobody kills someone over it, right?"

Somebody had, Martin thought, but was wise enough not to say it aloud. "Was your mother acting different at all this weekend? You notice any change yesterday?"

"No," Clarissa said. "She was gone all day yesterday. Dad was acting different. Well, not different, just quiet. He'd get like that sometimes."

"Sure," Martin said, giving her a sympathetic smile. "So your mom left in the morning to go into the store. You didn't see her before she left?"

Clarissa shook her head. "I didn't get up until after ten."

"Right. So she was at the shop all day and she didn't

come home last night, according to your dad."

"No. She had a meeting. And then she stayed with Aunt Karen." She paused after she said it, realizing that this could not have been what happened the night before, and Martin thought she was about to start crying again.

"Was that what she said she was going to do?"

"No. No. She didn't say anything." Clarissa hesitated, weighing her words. "That's just what she normally did, I know. We didn't worry about it."

"Okay," he said, deciding not to press her. If it came to it, he would re-interview her and force her to say what she had been going to. If he could avoid it, that would be a kindness. "Now, what about last night? It was just you and your dad here? Tell me what happened."

"I made Dad supper and then he got a call around seven or eight. I went upstairs and worked on my essay. I got ready for bed around eleven or so, and then stayed up chatting with some people until one or so."

"What time did your dad go to bed?"

Clarissa thought for a moment. "The lights were still on when I got ready for bed at eleven, which is a bit late for him, actually. I was listening to music, though, so I didn't hear when he went to bed for sure."

Martin thanked her for her time and went back downstairs. Leonard was sitting at the kitchen table with a cup of coffee in his hands, staring off into space. Martin had to clear his throat to get his attention.

"Get all that you need?"

"Yeah, thanks, Leonard," Martin said. "I'll probably have more questions as this goes on, but for now I'll leave you both."

Leonard nodded his thanks and Martin turned to go, but stopped himself. "Where did Kristi normally park her car? The garage?"

"Yeah," Leonard said with a careful nod.

"You don't mind if I take a peek before I go? Just need to exclude that from the investigation."

He could see several emotions flickering across Leonard's face all in the space of a few seconds, but in the end he just nodded and waved at Martin to go ahead. Martin gave him an apologetic smile, put on his jacket and boots, and headed out in the snow and cold. Before he returned to his car, he stuck his head in the garage to confirm that Kristi's car wasn't there. He had known it wouldn't be. Even if Leonard was involved in his wife's death, he was no fool.

As he returned to his car, the radio at his side crackled to life. "Dispatch to Loverna Detachment. Respond."

"Martin here," he said, after he had slipped into the car.

"We have a reported 10-81 at the UFA gas depot."

He sighed and put a hand to his head. It was just one thing after another. A robbery at the UFA. Somebody stealing gas again, no doubt. There had been five reported thefts in the last three months. He would pass by there on his way back into town so he could stop off and look things over. If it was similar to the last incidents, there would be little to see.

Having responded to the dispatch, he pulled out of the Taids' driveway and back onto the road, which by now had been entirely covered over with snow. He slowed as he passed by the coulee, wanting to make sure his makeshift crime scene was still in place. The impression left by Kristi's body had vanished, the snow rendering it invisible, but the pylons were still visible.

One of them had been knocked over, though, he assumed by the wind. He stopped the car and made his way across the road and down the ditch into the coulee to right it. When he came up to it, something about it made him go still. The pylon was too far from the other to have simply been knocked over the wind. Someone had moved it.

He knelt down to pick it up and return it to where he thought it should be. As he did, he saw what he had missed somehow on his descent: a set of footprints coming down from the ditch. He squinted through the snow to make sure they were not somehow his own from earlier, but these were fresher, and the soles of the boots were different. They were flat, without the grips that his own boots had, or those of Leonard's or Wayne's.

After staring at the tracks, trying to make sense of them somehow, he straightened up and began to follow them. The trail disappeared into the coulee below. He tried to peer through the snow to see if he could make anyone out hiding in the trees, but the snow would not allow it.

5

Martin contemplated descending into the coulee to find out who had passed that way, but he decided against it. Not without backup, not without anyone knowing where he was. Mayerthorpe, and the murder of his fellow officers, was always in his mind now, especially given he was in a town that was not so different than that, with many of the same problems to deal with. He followed the tracks back across the road through the other ditch and into the pasture on the other side of the road. It was Leonard's land, he thought. Evidently someone had thought the storm would be a good day for a walk.

Before starting on the long trip back into town, Martin stopped off again at the Johnstones' to see if they had noticed anyone passing by. They were both sitting in the kitchen, talking somberly over cups of coffee.

"I didn't see anyone, but hell, you could walk through the yard here and I might not notice you on a good day, let alone a day like today," Wayne said with a shake of his head.

"Any idea why someone would be heading down there?" Martin said.

Wayne shook his head. "You said they came from the

south off Leonard's quarter? Only folks in that direction are the Hutterites. Can't imagine why they would be out in a storm like this."

Martin could not either. He told them he would be back the next day, in all likelihood with a forensics team, and asked them to stay away from the area and to keep an eye to make sure no one tampered with it. When he was satisfied he had done all he could there, he set off at last for town.

It took him over an hour to return to Loverna, what was normally a twenty-minute drive transformed into an excruciating ordeal by the blizzard. The temperature, wavering around the freezing point at the beginning of the day, had left a sheen of ice beneath the steadily accumulating snow, making any speed above twenty kilometers an hour treacherous. Not that he could have gone any faster had he wanted to, for the wind and snow made visibility impossible. He had to stop twice to check in on some rigs that had slid off the road, but the drivers of both were fine, and preferred to wait out the storm and the tow truck in the comfort of their sleeping berths.

The highway passing by town was eerily quiet. He was surprised to see the road had not been plowed yet, and made a note to check in with the town office so see what had gone wrong there. Before he did that, he drove out east past the town proper to the intersection of Highway 9 and 41 where the UFA gas bar was.

The parking lot was full of drivers who had pulled off to wait out the storm. The Tumbleweed Diner, sitting next to the gas bar, was full to the brim as well. The hotels here and in town would be doing good business the next few days, he imagined. With the roads as they were, no one would be going anywhere.

He parked and headed into the gas bar. The young woman at the counter stood up at his entrance. Tammy was her name, if he recalled correctly. She'd been one of his first tickets, for open alcohol in a vehicle, when he'd staked out a high school party the year before. Martin thought she had graduated last year, but obviously she had yet to head off to school, as most of the area's young people did once they finished high school.

"You want me to get Gary for you?" she said, and Martin nodded.

She disappeared into the back, returning a moment later. "He'll just be a second. He's on the phone. Do you want some coffee?"

"Thanks, that'd be great." He waved her off as she moved to get him a cup, and went himself to the self-serve station at the back of the store. He was just mixing in some milk when Gary Seedstrom came out of the back. The UFA manager moved his chest upthrust, an easy, arrogant smirk perpetually upon his face, which looked younger than his forty odd years. He was small man in every way, or at least that was Martin's impression, though he couldn't say why he so disliked the man.

"You didn't have trouble getting here, did you?" Gary said as he shook Martin's hand. "Hell of a storm. Dispatch said you were out on another call."

"I was," Martin said, not offering any more. He wanted to see if he could keep word of Kristi's death hidden for as long as possible—a futile effort in this place, he knew.

"One of the truckers said they shut down Highway 9 too," Tammy said.

Martin nodded. "Big accident there between Hanna and Youngstown. With the storm, I imagine they'll keep it closed all day."

Gary shook his head. "Best to be safe, I imagine. Busy day for you, though."

You have no idea, Martin thought, but did not say. "So somebody got to the tanks again?" he said instead.

Gary grimaced. "Annoying as hell. Let me get my coat and I'll show you."

They went outside behind the gas bar, where the large storage tanks that held the bulk diesel and gas that was wholesaled to most farms and ranches in the area were situated. With the rise in prices above a dollar a liter in the last few years, there had been an increase in gasoline chicanery, which Martin had never imagined to police before moving out here.

Many farmers and ranchers tried to use the dyed gas— purple gas as it was known, which was discounted and intended for farm vehicles—in vehicles that weren't registered for farm use. Every few months Martin and Lara would set up a check stop, where they would test the gas in everyone's tank to make sure people were using the proper gas. Recently there had also been an upsurge in outright theft of gas, not only from the UFA depot, but the farms themselves. People had even started putting locks on tanks, which apparently was unheard of for the area.

As with the other incidents, the lock that stopped the handle opening the tank to the hose and nozzle from being turned had been cut. Someone had picked up the broken lock and hung it back on the handle, presumably to keep it from being lost in the snow, which had already begun to collect into a drift around the tanks.

"How much did they take?" Martin said.

"Figure about a tanker's worth," Gary said. "Same as before."

"You haven't set up the keypad access like I suggested?"

"It's on order. Guy said he'd be out next month," Gary said with a shrug.

"I imagine this might speed them up," Martin said, and Gary shrugged again, as though these were weighty matters beyond his control.

They returned inside to escape the snow, Martin pulling out his notebook and pen. "Any idea when this might have happened?"

"Last night, same as the others," Gary said. "We closed up around nine, like usual, and Tammy started around six."

"What time did you get here?" Martin said, turning to her.

"Be about five thirty, I guess," she said, nodding and eager to help. "Yeah, five thirty. I like to have time to get the coffee on and everything. And with the snow, I wanted to give myself extra time."

"It was already snowing when you got here?" Martin said.

"Oh yeah. It was already sticking to the ground, too."

"Did you notice any tracks?"

Tammy thought about it before shaking her head. "I don't think so. It was still pretty dark out, though. I could just as easily have missed them."

Martin asked a few other questions, but he knew what the answers would be before he said them, so he paid little attention, his thoughts already drifting to Kristi Taid's murder and all that needed to be done there. This would have to wait. He promised to look into the matter further, once the storm was through and he could attend to it. It was interesting, he thought as he returned to his car and started back for town, how little Gary had done to stop the thefts and how little he appeared to care.

6

The town Martin returned to seemed still in the depths of a heavy sleep. He encountered no cars as he made his way down First Avenue to the center of town. Judging by the tire tracks in the snow, it appeared only one or two people had gone before him. He felt as though he had returned to find himself in a post-apocalyptic movie, the town abandoned, but for the evil that lay in wait for him.

His first stop was on the north side of town, near the police detachment and his own home. At the center of one block there stood a vast—or at least what passed for vast here—cedar-walled home. It announced, in a way that few other houses here did, the wealth of those who lived there. Such ostentation was generally frowned upon in towns like Loverna, where people of all means went to the same stores and churches and knew each other's parents and cousins and secrets.

He slogged through the snow, guessing at where the sidewalk was, noting with incredulity that it was already past his ankles, and rang the doorbell. Even as he did, the door was being opened, and he was welcomed in by Karen Mahl, Kristi's sister. She was the eldest in the family, with Kristi the middle child and Kevin the youngest by a number of years.

She smiled as he thanked her and said hello, an involuntary gesture, her eyes red and puffy from crying.

"Sorry to bother you," he said. "I guess you've heard."

"Leonard called," she said. "Come on in. Can I get you a cup of coffee?"

"Sure, Karen, that would be great. I won't take much of your time. I just have a few questions."

"Of course," Karen said, as she poured him a cup of coffee and set it at the table along with milk and sugar. She looked, Martin realized, remarkably like her sister. Both were tall women who kept their hair cut short, as women out here seemed to. They had the same striking blue eyes that seemed to both pull and push the person on the receiving end of their gaze.

"Of course. I understand completely. I just can't really believe this has happened. I just saw Kristi yesterday."

"What time was that?"

"She stopped by for coffee in the morning. She always did when she was coming into town for the day, before she went to the Tea House."

Martin nodded, pulling out his notebook. "Did she seem herself?"

"Oh yes. I didn't notice anything the matter."

"Now." Martin paused, searching for the right way to phrase this. "Leonard mentioned that he wasn't surprised when she didn't come home last night. He said she often spent the night here when she had to stay late. Were you expecting her?"

"Constable," Karen said with a thin smile. "There's no need to play. I love my sister dearly, but I know what she is. That may have been the convenient fiction that existed between her and Leonard, but she never once spent the night here. And I did not expect her last night. I didn't see her, either."

She spoke very precisely and with firmness, as though she were addressing one of her students. It occurred to

Martin to ask if the school was closed with the storm or if she had taken the day off, but he realized it was of no consequence.

"Was there anything going on that you were aware of that had been bothering her?" Martin frowned, again seeking the right words. "Was there anyone who had reason to be angry with her?"

"Kristi was a difficult woman," Karen said. "I can say that as her sister. I don't think there was anything unusual about yesterday or the last little while. Anyway, there are difficult people everywhere, and Loverna certainly has no shortage of them. My father was difficult his whole life. But that's not enough to get one killed, I wouldn't think."

Martin nodded, though he did not agree. People had been killed for less—people had been murdered for nothing, in fact.

"And where were you last evening? I'm sorry, I have to ask everyone this."

"Not at all, Martin. I would expect nothing less than a proper investigation. I was here all night. I graded some assignments and then watched television."

"And how about Arnold?"

"He was here for supper early and then he went to the school board meeting. He went to the bar after—he and Ted often go for a drink after the meetings." Karen paused to reflect. "I went to bed early, around ten or so, I guess. I'm not sure what time Arnold got back, but it was later than I expected. I was already asleep."

There was a hint of displeasure in her voice, but it was distant, her mind elsewhere.

"Where is Arnold right now?" Martin said, closing his notebook and putting it in his pocket.

"I expect he's at work. They'll be open no matter the weather."

Martin thanked her for her time and the coffee and headed back out into the storm. He could feel her eyes upon him as he walked back to his car.

He stopped in at the town office, just off Main Street, to see why plowing had not started, and was told that there was a sewer problem that the two public works guys had to deal with before they could start on anything else.

"Not like anyone's coming into town on a day like today anyway," the girl at the office said, and he had to agree.

Both the public and Catholic schools were closed as well, she informed him, and while the drug and grocery stores were open on Main Street, that was only because the staff, for the most part, just had to walk down across town. Only the Hotel had trucks in front of it, the early coffee crowd having made their way there before the storm got too bad, no doubt planning to hunker down for the better part of the day now.

He drove past the Hotel, turning left onto Railway Avenue. The spur line that ran parallel to the road no longer saw any trains, and the elevators, those red and green skyscrapers of the prairies, had both been torn down before he arrived in town. A new elevator, concrete and massive, sat outside town now, the only one for an hour in any direction.

Past the Fountain Tire and a few other shops, the street turned residential, and he drove nearly to its end, where the town simply stopped and the fields stretched on as far as the eye could see. He pulled to a halt two doors down from where he wanted to go, though the driveway in front was open, hoping to stave off any rumors that might be started by his presence here. Those would come soon enough.

The call of the doorbell was answered by a series of curses and apologies. Martin waited, his back to the door, looking out on the empty street, enjoying for a moment the peaceful silence of the falling snow, at least here sheltered from the wind. The disheveled face that met his stare when he turned around did not betray any trace of surprise at seeing him.

"Martin," Tyler said. "Come on in."

He did, taking off his boots and jacket in the hall, Tyler leaving him there and retreating to the living room. Martin found him slumped into the couch, the coffee table in front of him littered with empty beer cans and a half-spent bottle of rye. The room stank of sweat and booze.

"Tied one on last night?" Martin said.

Tyler didn't answer, surveying the carnage that lay before him morosely. He had sad brown and deep-set eyes that, along with his shaved head, made him look older than his twenty five years. Like Cory, and so many of the other unattached men of that age in Loverna, he seemed to exist in a perpetual adolescence, devoting his life to work, drinking, hunting, and hockey.

"Know why you're here, man," he said at last. He stumbled over the words as he said them, then stopped as if realizing how he sounded.

"That so?"

"Yeah. Kristi's dead."

"That's right. So you understand I'm going to have to ask you some questions," Martin said, trying not to let his anger show. *Fucking Cory, can't keep his mouth shut for a goddamn hour.*

Tyler waved his hand for Martin to go ahead, still not looking up from the previous night's remains.

Martin swallowed. "When was the last time you saw Kristi?"

"Week ago."

"A week ago?" Martin said, with a raised eyebrow.

"That's what I fucking said, wasn't it."

"All right, all right. Was that normal?"

"No, it wasn't fucking normal," Tyler said, his hands clenching into fists. "What the fuck do you think? She was avoiding me."

"Why do you think she was avoiding you?"

"Well, I fucking know why."

Martin exhaled silently, careful not to let his frustration show. "Why, then?"

Tyler looked out the window, his lips working against each other to form silent words. Martin let the silence extend for what seemed a minute or more. "Do we need to take this down to the station?"

"The fuck, Martin? I didn't kill her," Tyler said, snapping his head around to face him.

"Nobody's saying you did."

"Why're you here, then, man, huh? Why else would you fucking be here?"

Martin let him cool down, sitting solid as a stone, letting the silence eat at him.

"She left me, all right?" Tyler said, throwing his hands up. "Said she didn't want to see me anymore. She never had the guts to leave him."

He seemed about to say more, but stopped himself. Martin gestured at the bottle on the table between them. "So you were still drowning your sorrows last night, then?"

"This," Tyler said with a laugh. "Richard and Russell and Cory stopped by last night. Got a bit out of hand."

"It happens. You stayed in, or did you go out?"

"We shut the Hotel down." He smiled to himself and then grew serious, leaning toward Martin. "Now, I'm not gonna lie: when—when I heard—I had a couple of sips. Had to. Had to. But I swear that's the truth of it."

Martin stood up, not taking his eyes off Tyler. "Fair enough," he said. "Now I've started an investigation, so I'll be talking to folks around town, trying to see who saw Kristi last. Before I do that, I'm going to give you one more chance, if you've got anything to add."

Tyler returned his gaze, and Martin nodded. "All right. I may have some questions for you as we go on here, so don't be making any trips out of town or anything."

Tyler laughed. "I fucking check oil wells, man. Where the fuck am I going in this shit?"

7

Outside the snow continued unabated, and Martin was left feeling tired and frustrated. There was no doubt in his mind that Tyler was lying about not seeing Kristi in the last week. Loverna was a town of thousand people, after all, and she ran one of the only restaurants.

The lie was pointless. It would only take asking around a little to find someone who could remember seeing them together, and then he would be back here again. Maybe Tyler would be sober by then and willing to talk sense, though Martin had his doubts.

He slipped into the car, slamming the door shut and reaching, by force of habit, into the glove box where he kept his cigarettes. There were none there. Lara had seen to that. The thought of her made him stop and close his eyes. Maybe he and Tyler were not so different, both entangled with women who were obviously too good for them. Women who were not theirs.

He had never known what it was Kristi had seen in Tyler, and nor, he suspected, did many others around town. In their few interactions, Martin had come away impressed by Leonard's intelligence and basic decency. Tyler, on the other hand, was a young man, even though he was in his thirties, and had on several occasions been at the center of incidents at the Hotel that had necessitated a call to the police.

Kristi Taid was out of his league, to put it plainly, though in the time Martin had been stationed here he had noticed a few of these uneven relationships; the result, he assumed, of lack of supply and a demand that would never diminish. But Kristi had done better, so why she would want to squander that with a well checker?

There was no reason to lust, he knew. People did what they did without thought or purpose, and only after tried to ascribe any sort of motive to it.

Why had Lara come to him, after all?

It did not bear thinking about, he knew, and he had mostly avoided doing so these last glorious months. Greg was a decent sort, an honorable man as far as Martin could tell, which was more than he could say for himself. But whether it was familiarity, boredom, or lust, something had drawn Lara to him. For himself, he knew what it was about her that had attracted him. She was intoxicating, sensuous, and yet sensible and practical, able to command any situation with ease.

He would feel so much more comfortable now if she were here to lead this investigation. But she and Greg had gone to British Columbia to see his family. Did he know, Martin wondered? Did he suspect at all? The questions worked at him like a dagger probing deeper and deeper.

They had not spoken about Greg at all, or about the longer term, whatever it might be. It was easy for Martin not to press her on the matter. Their relationship was still new, and he had no other entanglements, and desired no others in this town, where everyone seemed to know every last detail of everyone's business. It seemed an exhausting way to live.

Most of all, he did not want to force her to make any choice, because he was terrified he would lose.

He blinked, coming back to himself, and saw that the

snow had already blanketed all the windows on his car. He pulled the brush from the trunk and set to work at cleaning off the car while also trying to gather his thoughts. Tyler would no doubt be wondering why he had not left yet, as would anyone else who had noticed his presence, so it was time to get moving again, to start to piece this whole mess together. His first step should be Botha, to see if there was anything the doctor could tell him.

As he retraced his path back through town on his way to the hospital, he saw a truck he recognized parked in front of the Hotel and pulled over, heading into the diner. About half the tables and booths were occupied, he saw as he stamped the snow of his feet in the entryway. A smaller crowd than normal, but impressive given the storm. Lynn, the Chinese woman who ran the place with her husband, waved a greeting at him with a coffee pot in her hand.

"Any place you want," she said. "You want a coffee?"

"Please," he said, and made his way through the warren of tables, feeling the eyes of all those gathered upon him.

A silence followed in his wake, which meant word had already reached here. He saw why in a moment, as he made his way to where Russell Pedersson sat watching his approach with trepidation. He was tall and broad-shouldered, with a perpetual grazing of stubble that was starting to get speckled with grey.

As he came abreast of the booth, he saw that Cory was sitting with him, and he had to stop himself from rolling his eyes.

"Can I join you gentleman?" Martin said, pitching his voice loud enough so that everyone in the diner heard him.

Russell's eyes widened, and he looked as though he were debating whether to run right then or wait until Martin had sat down. Cory waved him in, sliding over to make room. "Of course, constable. You're always welcome at my table."

Lynn brought him his coffee and a cream packet. "Are

you eating with us today?"

He was about to say no, but at the mention of food he felt a pang of hunger. The clock showed the time as eleven thirty, which surprised him. Half the day gone and he was nowhere. He nodded at Lynn and looked at the board.

"I'll have the western special," he said, noting that she had not asked him how he was. The talk in the other booths had resumed, but at a low murmur, not the usual volume. It was going to be an interesting few days around town, he thought, resisting the urge to smile.

"You have any trouble getting back into town?" he said, turning to Cory.

"Nah, it was a bit messy out there. Botha said you could stop by this afternoon after three. He won't get to look at her until after lunch."

"Why is that?"

"I guess there's been a few accidents this morning," Cory said with a shrug. "At least one broken arm."

Martin nodded and looked at Russell, who was studying the fine details of his cutlery. "I guess you heard. I've started an investigation into Kristi Taid's death."

"I— Yeah, I heard," Russell said, looking at Cory, who nodded as though this were the first he were hearing of it as well. This time Martin could not resist a shake of his head.

"Well, I've got questions for you."

"Sure," Russell said.

"I was talking to Tyler just now. He said that you all were here drinking last night with him and Richard."

"That's right, we settled in for a spell," Russell said, his eyes still darting here and there.

"What time did you all get here?"

"I stopped by around eight or nine, I'd guess. These guys were already here."

Cory nodded and shrugged in agreement.

"And what time did you all leave?" Martin said, pouring and stirring the cream into his coffee without taking his eyes from Russell.

"Well, Cory and I stayed till about midnight or so. But Ty and Richard both left around ten or so, I'd say."

Martin was careful not to show any surprise. "Why was that?"

"Ty? He was pretty far gone already. Called it a night, I guess," Russell said with a nod.

"That right."

"Yep," Russell said, his eyes on the far side of the diner.

"He didn't say anything about Kristi last night, did he?" Martin said as Lynn brought plates of pork chops and potatoes for both Russell and Cory. Cory started in on his, but Russell did not move to pick up his cutlery.

"Oh, you know," Russell said. "He's been going on about that for a while now."

"Hmm," Martin said as he took a sip of coffee.

"So he went on about it last night too. You know, he was really drunk. Can't give much credit to what a man says when he's drunk." Russell was fingering his knife.

"Especially Ty," Cory said around a bite of potatoes.

"Yeah, the liquor does poor things to him," Russell said, a little too quickly. "Well, you know."

"That I do," Martin said. "Either of you see them together this past week?"

"Kristi and Ty?" Cory seemed confused. "No."

"Yeah, no," Russell said with a shake of his head. "She was always real careful, you know." He trailed off and looked away.

"Thanks, boys," Martin said.

Russell took that as a signal that he could start eating, which he did in earnest, refusing to look up from his plate at either Cory or Martin, who had to resist a smile. He turned his attention to Cory, who was oblivious to his stare.

"You hear about the gas thefts at the UFA the last couple of months?"

Cory appeared to consider the question. "A little, yeah, I think. Tankers of purple gas, right?"

"That's right. Every two weeks or thereabouts. Like somebody is making a shipment," Martin said, glancing over at Russell, who had gone very still again, his fork poised above his plate.

"Hm," Cory said. "Never thought about it like that. Guess you're right."

"Need a big truck to take that much gas."

"Yep," Cory agreed.

"How many trucks like that in the country?"

"Not many, I'd guess," Cory said. "I mean, Bill's got his and Richard has his. Russ, you've got yours. They all do deliveries for the UFA."

"Might be a few guys could put a tank on the back of their three-ton," Russell said. "Bit dangerous, though."

"You think it's somebody from around here, then?" Cory said, putting his fork down and pushing his plate away.

Martin shrugged. "Couldn't say, really. No evidence one way or the other."

Lynn arrived with his pork chops and mashed potatoes, and Martin accepted the plate from her with a smile and began to eat. Russell and Cory were silent, Cory watching him eat and Russell fidgeting in his seat.

"Listen," Russell said at last, "you mind if we…?"

"No, go ahead. Just don't go talking about what we discussed here. This is a police investigation. Things need to be kept confidential." Martin made sure to look at Cory as he said it.

The ambulance driver nodded in happy agreement. "Of course, of course," he said as Martin got out of his way and he and Russell left the booth.

Martin shook his head and took another bite of potatoes. Both of them were probably heading right to Tyler's to let him know he was a suspect. Not that it mattered. Everyone sitting in the diner now would be heading home to tell everyone they knew what they had seen, who he had been talking to, and guessing what about.

Martin pushed that annoyance aside and pulled out his pen and notebook. He started to assemble all that he knew about Kristi Taid's final hours. She had come into town first thing in the morning and spent the day at the Tea House, presumably. Carol would be able to confirm that, and his next stop would be there. She had the school board meeting at six thirty, and no doubt dozens of people would be able to confirm her presence there.

The meeting would have ended at eight, he guessed, so what had happened after that was the question that mattered. The Tea House closed early on Mondays, he thought, so it was unlikely she'd gone back there. He had assumed Kristi had spent the night with Tyler, but that was evidently not the case. Whom had she been intending to stay with if not him?

As he pondered these thoughts and listened to the murmurs of those around him, he realized there was a very good chance that someone in town knew what had happened last night and was not telling him. A shotgun going off would qualify as an unusual occurrence in town, as it wouldn't in the country, and it wasn't like people around here wouldn't recognize the sound for what it was. If his quick analysis of the body, and its cloudy eyes, was correct, then she had been killed between ten and one the night before, so enough people would have been awake to hear.

This all assumed she had been killed within the town limits, and he had nothing to suggest this was the case beyond his own gut feeling. He needed to find her car. That and establishing as much of a timeline for last night as he could manage were his priorities. Hopefully one or both of those would point him to where she had been shot, and that would suggest who had pulled the trigger on the shotgun.

He still had the feeling he was missing something. He

could only hope it was not crucial, though everything was crucial now. This was not stolen gas or lumber—this was life and death.

He finished his meal and coffee and left ten dollars on the table, ducking into the bathroom to relieve himself. It was the second time he had gone this morning, having stopped along the highway to color the snow on his trip back into town. Too much coffee, he needed to be careful. But the day would call for more before it was through, he felt certain.

Lynn waved at him as he left, but he barely noticed, his mind on all that needed to be done as he went back out into the storm.

8

Martin decided to walk rather than drive the block and a half to the Tea House. The wind swirled the snow as he went, mutating it into ghostly shapes that formed and vanished in an instant. There was no one the street as he walked, but a truck drove past, following in his earlier tracks, and all the stores were open, though it appeared as though there was no one inside any of them.

The Tea House was empty, but the young girl Sandra, who usually worked weekends, was at the front counter, a distant expression on her face, her eyes heavy and red. It took a moment for the girl to bring her focus to him, and Martin smiled in what he hoped was a consoling fashion.

What he was thinking, though, was that here was one benefit of being in a small town where word travelled quickly: he did not have to break the news to anyone.

"Schools are closed, I gather," he said to her, and she nodded. "Is Carol in?"

The girl nodded again and pointed to the back, where the kitchen was. He smiled his thanks and then asked her, "You didn't happen to be around here last night, did you?"

She shook her head and looked as though she was about to start crying again. He waved at her and went into the kitchen, where he found Carol Hargreaves mixing ingredients into a batter. He cleared his throat as he came in, and she looked up from her work in surprise.

"Oh," she said, and returned to mixing. Martin watched her as she added flour to the mixture she had, the smell of bananas and vanilla strong in the air, and began to incorporate it. She worked with a barely contained intensity, her long blonde hair pulled back into a ponytail. Always thin she seemed almost frail now as Martin studied her, though he knew that was deceptive. She was not someone to be crossed, if rumors were to be believed.

Nor was Kristi, if those stories were to be believed as well. They were quite similar, in so many ways, at least from what little Martin knew of the two of them. Both were in their early forties and had married young and had children who had already left home. They had taken the extra time afforded by their children getting older to start the Tea House, as well as getting involved in the community in various ways, including the school board.

By all accounts things the Tea House had been a great success. There were so few restaurants in town—the Hotel, the diner by the highway gas bar, and the Chinese restaurant were the only others—that it filled a need, especially with so many oil workers regularly passing through. But was that the whole story, or had there been tensions between the two willful owners? He recalled Leonard's words: *Good as can be expected.* What did that mean exactly?

"I don't even know why I'm bothering," Carol said to him without looking up. "I should just close and send Sandra home. Nobody's going to be in with the storm, and…"

"Probably good to keep yourself busy," Martin said. "A day like this. Where's Lyle at?"

She made a vague gesture with her hand but didn't answer. The batter mixed to the consistency she wanted, she emptied the bowl into a bread pan, scraping it clean with a spatula and then smoothing out the loaf.

"I suppose you'll be wanting to ask me some questions," she said as she put the tray into the oven.

"I'm afraid so," he said. "I'm trying to put together what she was doing last night."

"Well, she had the school board meeting last night. We were both there, actually. It went until eight thirty, nine. Then we came here."

"Why'd you come here?" he asked, watching as she washed her hands and then started to roll out some pie dough that had been warming on the counter.

"Oh, we had a few things to finish up. Made sense to do them last night, since she was in town, rather than today, with the storm coming." She stopped, holding the rolling pin over the dough, as though confused by what she had said.

"How long were you here for?"

"Probably an hour or so. Honestly, I couldn't say. It was late enough, anyway. When we were leaving, Tyler came by, drunker than anything. You should arrest him for drunk driving. I can't believe that."

"What happened when he came by? Where was he?"

"Oh, we were just out back," Carol said, pointing behind her to the alley. "We were both parked out there. He kind of pulled up, blocked us off, and then got out and started yelling at Kristi."

"What'd he say?"

She made a motion with her hand, like such things were beneath her. "Oh, I try to stay out of Kristi's life. Not my choices."

"But you heard what they said?"

"Yeah. Tyler wasn't making much sense. He couldn't even stand straight, for God's sake."

"He was that drunk?" Martin said, frowning. He was not surprised; he couldn't count the number of times he had dragged Tyler or Russell or Cory out of the Hotel bar so drunk they could barely stand. What did surprise him was Carol's lack of emotion. She seemed more perturbed at Kristi's death, as if it were just another annoyance to be suffered, like her choice in men.

"Oh yes. Just making a fool of himself. Not that there's anything strange about that. But that's not my business either."

She had finished rolling out the dough, and now laid it across the bottom of a pie plate, gently pressing it into form. That done, she turned to the fridge and pulled out a bowl of cut apples, pouring them over the dough and smoothing the edges. They were stained with cinnamon and brown sugar.

Martin watched her work, and when the pie was done and in the oven, he pressed her again. "What did they say?"

Carol hesitated and then said, "Well, he did threaten her."

"To kill her?" Martin said.

"Not in so many words. Just threatened her, right. I mean, he wasn't making any sense, really, but I was scared. He was so angry at her."

"Because she'd broken it off with him?"

"Yes," she said with a sigh.

"So what happened?" Martin said.

"Well, Kristi wouldn't take the bait. She just told him to go home and sleep it off. I was worried, though, so I went in and phoned Lyle. I thought he should follow Kristi home, just to make sure, you know, that nothing happened. Because even if Tyler didn't mean anything by it, he was so drunk that who knows what he was thinking. By the time I came back out, Tyler had left and Kristi went home."

"She didn't wait for Lyle?"

"No, she didn't seem too worried about it. I told her I'd called Lyle, but she just thought I was overreacting." Carol shook her head, pursing her lips in thought, thinking, no doubt, that if she had done something different, Kristi might still be alive.

Martin thanked her, telling her he might stop by later that night with some questions, and to talk with Lyle as well.

"You don't want a treat before you go?" she said, gesturing at the oven, where the pie and banana bread were baking. "It'll probably just go to waste."

Martin declined with a shake of his head and a smile. "Oh, I imagine you'll be busy enough the next few days with the funeral and everything else coming up. That stuff will get used."

He left, heading back out the front, giving the young girl a nod as he passed and then ducked back into the storm.

9

Martin checked his watch as he made his way back through the snow to his car and saw that he had over an hour until Botha would be ready. Time enough to head back to Tyler's and get that out of the way. He was more likely to find out something useful there as well, since he didn't expect Botha to find anything that he didn't already know, unless the doctor had been a forensics wizard in South Africa. Botha had many surprises, in Martin's experience, but he doubted that was one of them.

He had to clean the snow off the car again, which irritated him for some reason. When he sat in the car he felt the weight of exhaustion settle upon him, and closed his eyes. He desperately wanted another cup of coffee, but he resisted going back into the Hotel restaurant. It would only set him on edge now. A cigarette was what he really wanted, but he told himself he couldn't do that. He had promised Lara.

Nothing had prepared him for this. All the training had come back to him from the moment he had seen the body, and he had known what needed to be done. Even now he knew what he had to do, the steps he needed to take. But he did not feel in control of the situation. Far from it.

He was constantly left with the sense that there was so much that remained obscure and beyond his grasp. Though the evidence now seemed to point in Tyler's direction, and Martin's instincts from the first had suggested the same, he did not quite trust them. He still felt that he was missing something important.

That something, he realized, was at least in part Kristi herself. What did he know about her, really? Their every conversation had always had that mask of small-town friendliness that so many people used here as their armor against a stranger such as himself. A pleasant conversation, filled with smiles, that somehow kept him firmly on the outside as someone who would not be here for long, someone whose roots did not go back one hundred years or more. That was his fate here with most people, one that he had accepted. After all, he would be gone in after years, on to another town.

He forced these thoughts away and drove back to Tyler's house. This time he did not bother with subterfuge, parking out front. Let people say what they would.

"Oh Christ," Tyler said when he answered the bell. He looked to have moved on to a hangover, though Martin suspected he wouldn't linger there long.

"Can I come in?"

"You got a warrant?"

"I don't need a warrant," Martin said. "I'm not here to look around. I just want to talk."

"I think we did that already," Tyler said, stepping back and letting him in. "Fuck, the neighbors'll be wondering what the fuck I did last night."

"Them and me."

"Jesus, man. I told you, didn't I?" Tyler said, his throat sounding raw. "No offense—I mean, I enjoy your fine company, constable—but I've got myself a bit of headache that I'd like to wear off before I deal with anybody else today."

"You told me a lot of things," Martin said, ushering

Tyler into the kitchen. There was half a pot of coffee left, and he helped himself without asking, getting the milk from the fridge and giving it a sniff before he poured it in.

"But then I talked to Russell," he continued, "and he told me some things too. And the things he told me don't jibe with the things you told me, so you'll understand my confusion."

Tyler's face fell at those words. Martin held the coffee pot up to see if he wanted any, but Tyler shook his head, biting his lip.

"So," Martin said, sitting down. He took a sip of coffee, already regretting that decision, and leveled his gaze at Tyler. "Let's try again, shall we."

Tyler nodded. "All right, all right. I shouldn't have fucking lied, but I just wasn't thinking straight, you know."

"Russell said you left the bar around ten."

"Yeah, that could be," Tyler said with a shrug. "Honestly, I was wrecked, so I'm not really sure."

Martin held his gaze for a moment, looking for something in his expression, though he couldn't say what. "Then what?"

"Well." Tyler exhaled. "I walked home. Well, I was on my home, anyway. I went past the Tea House, you know, and saw the lights on. And I just thought I'd see if she was in."

Martin pulled his notebook out and clicked his pen. "And she was," he said.

"Yeah," Tyler said. "Yeah, she was. Her and Carol."

"So what happened then?"

"Man, I walked into a real rhubarb. I don't know what was going on, but they were both in the kitchen, yelling and screaming at each other."

"Carol and Kristi?"

"Who the fuck else?" Tyler said, raising his hands.

"You even remember what happened last night?" Martin said, unable to stop himself.

"Hey, I'm not saying all the scenes are there, or even

that they're in the right order. But that I remember, no doubt I remember."

"All right. What were they fighting about, then?"

"Oh, you know, the usual. Kristi wanted Carol out. And Carol wanted Kristi out. Or they both wanted to burn the place down, rather than let the other one have it. Been talking about it for months."

"Really," Martin said, recalling how Carol had looked when he talked with her. The lack of emotion, the annoyance with Kristi. People expressed their grief in different ways, he knew, and just because Carol was not flailing around in tears was no proof of anything. Lying to him was, though.

"Oh yeah." Tyler nodded vigorously. "I even heard she was going to get Gary to raise the rent on the Tea House so they couldn't afford it. Then Carol would leave and she could go back in on her own."

"Why would Gary do that?" Martin said with a frown.

Tyler shrugged. "Fucked if I know. Maybe she was fucking him too."

"What makes you say that?"

"I seen them around together a lot." Tyler hesitated on the last word and Martin wondered what *a lot* constituted.

Martin leaned back in his chair, setting his pen across his notebook. "You'll have to forgive me here, but given our talk this morning, I have my doubts about what you're telling me."

"Why? You don't think Kristi was that kind of person? I knew her, man," Tyler said, jabbing his finger into the table to emphasize his words. "She wasn't what you think at all."

"That so?"

"Yeah." Tyler looked away, now tapping his hand on the kitchen table.

"Who told you about the deal between Gary and Kristi for the Tea House?"

Tyler still wouldn't meet his eyes. "Cory."

Martin resisted the urge to snort. "So they were fighting. You come in, and what happened then?"

Tyler didn't answer for a moment, still gazing off into the next room. Finally he turned back to Martin, leaning forward across the table to look him in eye. "Man, look, I know how it looks. I know. I was fucking drunk last night. Full out. Couldn't walk a line if you let me crawl it, but I could never, never do a thing to her."

"That right?"

Tyler smiled, though there was no happiness in it. "Maybe you don't know what I'm talking about, but maybe you do. I cared about her so much, but at the end of the day I was just the guy she had fun with. She was never leaving him for me."

Martin felt his jaw go tight, and he had the sudden urge to walk out, back to the storm. How many people knew about he and Lara? The thought left him ill. If an idiot like Tyler knew then Greg knew too. He wanted to punch something or someone. Instead he said, "Seems like there's a lot of after-the-fact explaining going on here, but nothing that explains what happened last night."

"Like I said, I walked in there. They were fighting. Kristi could tell right away I was three sheets, and she told me to get the hell out."

"So you left?"

"I did," Tyler said, nodding. "I always did what Kristi said."

Martin got up and left, not even bothering with an explanation or a goodbye.

"We good, constable?" Tyler called after him as he slid on his boots.

"We'll see," was all Martin could bring himself to say. He wanted it to sound like a portent of doom, but it came out more as a question, as though he too had no idea what was about to happen. Which was the truth, but it was no comfort to either of them.

10

It was close enough to three that Martin decided to head to the hospital to see if Botha had finished with his examination. He was left cooling his heels in one of the waiting rooms for half an hour as the doctor dealt with someone who had slipped and broken an ankle in the storm. He contemplated the blizzard as he did so, wondering if perhaps it was abating some as the afternoon wore on. The swirling wind, which cast the falling snow about in all directions, suggested otherwise, though. What a day, he thought. What a goddamn day.

When Botha was finally able to see him, he had nothing to tell him that Martin hadn't already figured out for himself. That was no surprise, and yet Martin had hoped that somehow he was wrong and that Botha would discover something he had missed. It should have been a comfort that his observations and judgment had been sound, but instead all he could think about was that everything was now up to him. Kristi's murderer would be found or not based on his efforts and his alone.

The road into town from Hanna was still closed in the aftermath of the accident and the continuing storm. According to the dispatch, someone from there or

Youngstown might make it in by tomorrow afternoon, if the weather cleared tonight and nothing else happened. The same was true of the forensics team, although at this point Martin doubted they would be of much help. He needed to find where Kristi had been murdered for them to be any use, and he was still not any closer to doing that.

Although it was early still, he decided to head back to the barracks and put together some supper, with maybe a little nap first. The efforts of the day had exhausted him, and the coffee at Tyler's place had only given him a headache. Or maybe it was just the man himself who had. He lay down for half an hour, during which his mind would not let him drift off as he continually went over and over where things stood and what remained to be done.

He needed to canvass the street to see if anyone had noticed when Tyler had returned home, and whether it had been on foot or driving. It was unlikely, but there was always a chance. He also had to talk to Lyle, so that he could hopefully make sense of what both Tyler and Carol had said. One of them had to be lying. And he needed to find Kristi's car. Wherever it was might point in the direction of the crime scene.

Beyond that, who was there still to question? Martin needed to see if Kristi had in fact intended on spending the evening with Karen and if she had ever arrived. And if not, where was she going to go? Martin suspected Carol might be able to shed some more light there.

There was Kevin as well, the younger brother. Martin knew there was something between them, or at least he had heard something to that effect. Not uncommon out here, as he understood, squabbles between families over who was to get what on the family farm. So that certainly was worth inquiring about. Beyond that, he was at a loss.

When he was through trying to sleep, he got up and reheated some of last night's dinner, an uninspiring stew he had attempted. It was no better now, though it hardly mattered. His thoughts were elsewhere as he ate, unable to let go of the details of the case or Tyler's words to him.

"Maybe you don't know what I'm talking about, but maybe you do."

He was just talking, trying to get cast suspicion away from himself, desperate to. He meant nothing by it. Probably. But Martin was not sure. The thought that Tyler, that others, might know about he and Lara gnawed at him. The fear that lay at the heart of him was why he couldn't let it go.

If Lara knew that their affair was known in the community, would she end it? She probably would, Martin knew. She was exceedingly practical in everything, and she would see, as he could see now, how the town knowing about them could cause them problems down the line, both here and with the RCMP brass.

The sensible thing, with any affair, was always to end it, as Kristi had done with Tyler. As Lara, he felt certain, would do with him.

Dusk was settling across the horizon, when Martin at last emerged from his house to return to the task at hand. The sky was still heavy with clouds from the storm, though the snow had dwindled for the moment to a steady trickle. He could now see to the outskirts of town as he drove back to Main Street. The wind had died as well, a calm settling over everything, along with a deep stillness that seemed to extend for miles.

He passed Bruce out plowing the street, which meant the plumbing issue had finally been dealt with. It would be a late night for him as well. Martin drove to the end of the street where the Hotel was and was unsurprised to see a few vehicles parked out front. The diehards for the bar, no doubt.

He turned to the right and went around back where there was some more parking tucked behind the building. Two trucks were parked there, both covered in snow. Martin contemplated them for a moment, thinking about the stories Carol and Tyler had told him. Carol had said Ty had driven to the Tea House, while Ty had claimed he had walked. Hard to say who was telling the truth, unless Ty had driven to the bar and not bothered to get his truck back today.

Martin got out of the car, leaving it idling, the lights illuminating the two vehicles. He brushed the snow from the hood of each, using his forearm. One was green and one was blue. Neither was Tyler's vehicle. Martin pursed his lips and returned to his car. There would be no easy answers for him today, it seemed.

He turned back onto Main Street and headed for the Tea House. It was already dark, as were most of the other shops, there being no point in staying open with no one coming into town. He drove around back to check to see if Kristi's car was still parked there. Somehow he had forgotten to check earlier, not that he expected to find anything. If Carol had been lying about Kristi leaving, she surely would have thought to move her car somewhere.

He stopped in the alley behind the building, which looked very square and anonymous, no different than any of the others on the block without the false fronts to distinguish them, his headlights illuminating the parking stalls where the Tea House staff parked. Kristi's car wasn't there, but there were tracks leading away from one of the stalls, presumably from Carol's car. He was about to drive away when something on the white trim of the doorframe caught his eyes. He grabbed his flashlight and walked up to building to take a closer look.

There was no need for the flashlight, for as soon as he came close to the door he could see that it was pellet spray from a shotgun. Bringing the flashlight to bear on the brown of the building and the door, he could see other holes where the shotgun pellets had embedded themselves. For a moment he stood in disbelief, his mind unwilling to process what he was seeing. Then he began to swear before re-collecting himself and retreating to the car for a plastic bag and some pliers.

He dug out what he could from the wall, the flashlight in his mouth to provide a guiding light. In one of the holes he found the true prize, a strand of hair taken with one the pellets. He could see no other traces of Kristi's body, and some digging through the snow around where he thought she would have been standing revealed nothing either. He spent some more time looking for the shell casing, but that too was nowhere to be seen. Someone had taken the time to clean up what they could, and the snow had done the rest.

It was fully dark by the time he was done in the alley and the weather had turned cold. He had to huddle in the car for a bit to regain his warmth. As he did, he considered his next steps and watched as the snow continued to fall.

11

When Carol saw it was him at the door, she did not look surprised. Martin thought he saw something like resignation cross her face, replaced by a thin smile as she welcomed him in.

"It's Martin, Lyle," she called out as he took off his boots in the entryway. "He's probably got some questions for us. Can I get you anything?"

"Thanks," he said. "I'll be all right."

She led him to the kitchen, where Lyle was sitting finishing a plate of spaghetti. He looked up, with the ready smile he always wore, which, along with the thick tangle of his hair, made him seem more youthful than his forty seven years. "Sorry, Martin. Bit late getting in tonight."

"I apologize for the intrusion," Martin said.

"Not at all. Not at all," Lyle said with a firm shake of his head. "Completely understandable. Must have been a hell of a day for you."

Martin smiled to put him at ease, and a glance from Carol returned him to his plate.

"So I just have a few questions and I'll be out of your hair," Martin said, sitting down at the table across from Lyle. Carol remained standing, hovering between Lyle and the entry to the living room, as though she might flee at any moment. "Now, Lyle, what time did Carol phone you last night?"

Lyle looked startled. "Oh. I'd say 'round ten or so."

Martin pulled out his pen and notebook. He jotted something down and then looked up at Lyle. "What'd you do?"

"Well, uh, I went right over, you know. She said that, uh, Ty was threatening Kristi."

"That surprise you at all?"

"No," Lyle said, waving his fork. "You know how he gets."

"True enough," Martin said.

"You talked to Ty yet?" Carol said. "Sorry, I know I shouldn't ask a thing like that."

"No, no," Martin said with an understanding smile. "I have. That's partly why I'm here. Just trying to get all the details confirmed. You understand."

Carol nodded, though she did not appear reassured. "Sure you don't want anything? I'm going to make myself some tea."

Martin shook his head. "Now just to be clear on what happened here, Carol: Ty shows up and blocks you guys from leaving with his truck. He and Kristi get into it, and you go call Lyle. Now, Lyle, you head over to see what's going on."

They nodded in unison.

"Now, Tyler had gone by the time you got to the Tea House?"

"Oh yes," Lyle said with a vigorous nod.

"And you went right over after Carol called you?"

"Of course."

Martin nodded, his eyes on Lyle, though he could feel Carol watching him. "And Kristi had gone too?"

"Yes." Lyle glanced at Carol as he said it.

Martin noted that, looking from face to face, and nodded to himself. "So, what did you do then?"

"Well, we debated a bit about going after Kristi," Lyle said.

"I thought he should," Carol said, interrupting him. "I was worried Ty was going to do something."

"But I didn't think so," Lyle said with a shrug. "Hope I wasn't wrong. He talks a lot of nonsense, you know, and he does a lot of stupid things, but I don't think he's a bad guy in the end. At least not someone capable of that."

Martin nodded. *No one is capable of murder—until they are.* He made a show of writing something else in his notebook before closing it. "Well, I won't take any more of your time tonight," he said. "I know it's been a hard day. I may have some questions for you as we move this thing along."

"Anything, Martin," Lyle said. "Anything at all, uh, just a terrible thing."

Martin nodded and stood up. Carol stepped toward him. "Do you have any leads about who did it? Can you tell us?"

"Well, I can't say much about that, obviously. The investigation's still ongoing. But I've made good progress today. Tomorrow I'll hopefully have a forensic team coming in to look for evidence." He hesitated, as though considering whether to say more, before continuing. "Somebody called in saying they spotted her car, so, assuming the roads have been plowed, we'll get that and they can have a look and see what they've found."

Both of them went very still, the blood going from Carol's face. Martin was careful to keep his own expression impassive. He went out to the hallway and started to put on his boots. Carol and Lyle trailed behind him, Carol unconsciously working her hands together.

"Why would they find anything in her car?" Carol said with a frown.

"Well, she wasn't killed where we found her. So they obviously had to move her. I would assume they used her car to do that since they wouldn't want to leave her car at the scene of the crime," Martin said, looking up at them.

"She was a pretty bad mess, I'm sorry to say. You couldn't clean it up, not enough to hide from a forensics team, anyway. In all likelihood that's where we'll find our proof of who did it too. A hair, a fingerprint, a bit of cloth. You just don't catch it all. Not unless you really know what you're doing."

He stopped and looked at both them. "Sorry, I shouldn't be saying this. You don't want to be hearing any of it. Sorry to bother you this evening."

They both wished him good night and watched him out the door. Martin went to his car and drove away down the street, turning at the corner and doubling back around. He didn't turn back onto their street, stopping on the one perpendicular to it. He slid his car out of sight behind Aaron Gosgrove's truck beneath the shadows of a weeping larch bowed with snow, and switched the engine off.

The only streetlight was a block away, which he thought would help to hide him better in the event someone drove past, as he expected them to shortly. The Hargreaves' house was beyond his vision in the middle of the street, but he would be able to hear any car driving on any of the streets nearby. If someone left from their street, heading out of town, it would most likely be in this direction, and he would be able to follow.

After a moment his headlights went off, and he was left to wait in the darkness and the growing cold of the night. The snow had stopped falling, though the sky was still dark with clouds, not a star shining through above.

12

Martin waited nearly twenty minutes, the cold gradually seeping into his bones, before he heard the truck's engine on the other street. He had almost begun to doubt his hunch and wonder if he had missed some vital clue at the Tea House, though he knew he had not. The low and distant rumble of the diesel engine and the odd crunch of rubber on snow as the truck began to move came as a great relief. From where he sat he could see the lights of the truck as it drove by along the Hargreaves' street, but little of the vehicle itself, certainly not enough to identify it or who was driving it.

As he rolled down the window, he could hear the vehicle heading south to the 899 highway, and he knew that one or both of Carol and Lyle would be the only ones daring the roads tonight. They had to, for they believed their plan was unraveling with the discovery of Kristi's car. They would have to move the car, or get rid of it somehow. At any rate, that was where they were heading, and they would be taking Martin right to it.

He started his own car and pulled out onto the street, heading down to where it intersected with the highway. He sat for a moment looking to the west, where he could see the truck's headlights, beacons in the darkness, waiting until they disappeared along the horizon before turning out onto the highway. The last thing he wanted was to give them any reason to panic, which his lights in their rearview mirror might. The truck was the first vehicle on this road in hours, and so its tracks were fresh and obvious. He would not have an issue following them.

The going was slow, even with the Hargreaves having broken the trail ahead of him. The amount of snow that had accumulated in one day was incredible. He had never seen anything quite like it. It was up to his knees at least, and if not for the truck ahead of him, there was no chance his car would have been able to make it. Even still it was touch and go, and he worried about what would happen if they went off the highway and onto a gravel road.

The tracks continued to the intersection with the 570 about two miles west, where the truck turned north. Another vehicle had passed by that way earlier, so the going was a little easier, but now Martin had to worry about determining which tracks to follow. If he was lucky, the second vehicle was not driven by a local, though that seemed unlikely given the storm.

Every now and again he caught a glimpse of the Hargreaves' lights somewhere ahead of him on the road, which meant they would be able to see his lights as well. He was far enough behind them, he hoped, that they would not suspect he was following them. There was no one else on the highway aside from the two of them, unsurprising given the state of the road. It was agonizingly slow going, the car struggling through the snow, and nerve-racking as he fought to keep the wheels on the tracks carved for him.

Eventually he came to the intersection of 570 with Highway 41. One set of tracks continued north, while the other turned west. Without hesitation, he turned west. The Johnstones', where the body had been discovered, was only a few miles on. It would make sense that the vehicle would have been dumped somewhere nearby, given the apparent rush they had been in to dispose of her.

The tracks went past the Johnstone place, and he followed the curve of the highway past the coulee, where the body had been discovered, toward the Taid homestead. His eyes searched to the limits of the headlights and saw where the tracks turned ahead into the Taids' driveway. He was still absorbing that, and not paying enough attention to the road as it began to straighten, when he lost control of the car. He knew enough not to touch the brakes, though that was his first instinct, and tried to turn into the skid and then against it. Nothing he did mattered, and the car went headlong into the ditch.

"Fuck me," he said in an even voice, surprising himself. What the hell did he do now?

Though it seemed as though he was only on the edge of the ditch and not that far down into it, when he tried to reverse, the tires spun and refused to grab. His headlights were nearly covered in snow, the front of the car engulfed in a snowbank. He got out to investigate further, taking a step toward the front of the car, and immediately sank into snow up to his waist.

After digging his way free, he went to the trunk and pulled out the shovel, checking to make sure there was a bag of sand as well. Before he started to shovel the car out, he peered through the darkness at the Taids' yard. Though there were a few yard lights atop power poles to provide illumination around the cattle pens, he could not see where the Hargreaves' truck was parked through the trees. It did not appear to be parked in front of the house, but he could not say for sure.

Before he started to dig, he contemplated what his next steps should be. If he couldn't manage to get the car out, his options would be very limited. He would have to call someone—the Johnstones, the Taids, or the Mzikevitches—to come and pull him out. No matter who he asked, it would not escape the attention of whoever was on the Taids' ranch right at this moment, so maybe better to call Leonard directly, even if Martin was still unsure of what he might be walking into. It was a risk, there could be no doubt, but he needed to find out where Kristi's car was, or determine what exactly had brought the Hargreaves out here.

He made his decision and started to dig out the car. Once he was done, he put out some sand under the tires, got in the car, and turned off the engine. He called into dispatch and notified them of what he was doing, asking for Kevin Mzikevitch's phone number. Laureen answered on the second ring.

"Laureen? Martin Thomas here," he started.

"If this is about Kristi, we haven't spoken in five years," Laureen said.

Martin cleared his throat. "I understand, but I still need to ask you and Kevin some questions."

There was silence on the other end, and then he heard her calling for Kevin. "Hello?" he said.

"Constable Thomas here, Kevin," Martin said as Laureen told him who it was. "Like I was telling Laureen, I just need to ask you folks a few questions about your sister."

"Terrible news," Kevin said in a quiet voice. "But we haven't spoken in five years."

"I understand, but this is procedure in these cases, so I'm going to have to ask you."

There was a moment's pause before Kevin spoke again. "Sure. Ask away."

"Actually, I'm out near your place right now. Is it all right if I swing by?" Martin said.

"Out in this?" Kevin said. "You're a braver man than I."

"Stupider may be the word for it," Martin said. "I'm in the ditch right now. I'm just about to get Leonard to pull me out, and I'll be over to your place after."

"We'll keep an eye out for you, then. Let me know if

you guys need any help getting the car out."

Martin thanked him, hung up, and got out of the car. It had begun to snow again, though only lightly. Somewhere behind him a coyote howled mournfully. Another responded from even farther away, along with the yips of a couple of foxes very near to where he stood. A thought occurred to him as he looked back along the road to where the coulee began, and he pursed his lips. He had a good idea whose footprints those had been across the crime scene, but that would have to wait for the morning.

For now he had bigger problems to face. He started walking toward the Taids', the crunch of his footsteps sounding loud now that the coyotes and foxes had quieted. As he came down the driveway past the caraganas that lined the road, he could see the Hargreaves' truck sitting out front. There were lights on in the house, and he went to the front door.

13

Leonard answered the door looking mildly surprised. "Is there something I can help you with, constable?"

Martin smiled. "Sorry to bother you again, Leonard. Do you mind if I come in for a minute and warm myself up? I got myself stuck in the ditch, unfortunately, and just spent half an hour trying to get myself out."

"Sure. Of course," Leonard said, stepping aside to allow him to enter. He looked exhausted, Martin realized, as though the weight of the whole day was coming home to rest on him.

"Can I get you something to drink? We're just having some tea here."

"No, no," Martin said. "I don't want to stay long. I just wanted to stop by and warm myself up and see if I could get you to phone over to the Johnstones and see if Wayne can help me get my car out."

"It's no problem. I can help you."

"I don't want to bother you with this, Leonard," Martin said with a firm shake of his head. "Besides, you've got company."

As he said the word, Lyle emerged from the kitchen, giving Martin a nervous smile. "Constable. I thought we were the only ones stupid enough to be on the road tonight."

Martin chuckled. "It was ambitious of me, looks like."

Lyle nodded. "What brought you out here, if I can ask? I thought you were waiting for the forensics team tomorrow."

He seemed agitated, Martin thought, though he was working hard to control it. Carol had not appeared, and he wondered if she was in the kitchen. Briefly, he considered asking for a cup of tea just to find out, but decided against it.

"That will have to wait for tomorrow," he said, not specifying what that was. "I wanted to come back out and check on the crime scene tonight. I saw some footprints around it after we took the body away this morning, and I wanted to see if there were more tonight."

"Who could that have been?" Leonard said. "Wayne and Diane would have mentioned if they saw someone stopping out there while we were talking."

"I have some ideas," Martin said, not offering any more. He turned to Lyle. "What brings you out here on a night like tonight?"

He tried to make it sound like idle conversation, but Lyle flinched at the question. "We just didn't want to make Leonard and Clarissa have to spend the night alone, I guess. Seemed important that somebody be here, you know."

"Sure," Martin said, rubbing his hands together.

It made sense for the Hargreaves to be here, he realized. Leonard's parents had both passed on and his other sibling, a sister or brother, Martin couldn't recall which, lived in Edmonton. There was no close family here to look on him, not with Kristi feuding with her brother. Karen, perhaps, though maybe that relationship was strained as well.

"Well, I should give Wayne a call," Martin said as the silence became awkward. "I phoned Kevin and said I would stop by and ask him a few questions tonight too."

Leonard looked sharply at Martin. "You don't think he had anything to do with this, do you?"

"It's routine to talk to close family and friends in this situation," Martin said.

"Of course," Leonard said in a dull voice.

Martin peered at him. Did Leonard not want him talking to Kevin? It appeared so.

"You know what, rather than bothering Wayne, why don't I come out and give you a hand?" Lyle said. "Leonard, you should be with your daughter right now."

Martin acquiesced, in part because he wanted the opportunity to talk with Lyle alone, away from Carol. They headed outside, going back behind the house and down the hill to where Leonard had said the quonset that held the tractors was. It was a long building, shaped in a half-cylinder, with large hangar doors they had difficulty getting open from the snow. They needed to combine their efforts, both grunting and swearing until the snow gave way and they were able to open the door wide enough for a tractor to get out.

Lyle found the lights, which flickered dimly to life, the fluorescents needing time to warm up. There were two tractors parked right at the front of the building, with a bailer and a combine parked behind, obscuring the vehicles behind that. Lyle marched right to the first tractor and Martin followed reluctantly behind, trying and failing to find a reason to wander through the whole building to see if Kristi's car had been stowed here.

There was a set of chains on the floor of the cab, which Lyle checked before starting to ensure they would work. Martin stood on the steps leading into the cab as Lyle guided the tractor out of the quonset, increasing the throttle and shifting up the gears. They made their way past the house and out the driveway to the highway, where Martin's car sat partially buried in the snow.

Neither of them said a word until they were out of the

tractor and hooking the chains between the two vehicles.

"Hell of a day for you," Lyle said as they tested the chains to make sure they held to the car.

Martin nodded. "Yeah, not what I expected when I got up this morning. What can you tell me about Kristi, by the way? What was she like? I didn't know her, really."

"Doesn't feel like I did either, to be honest," Lyle said with a shake of his head. He looked up in the sky at the snow that continued to float slowly to the earth.

"Carol will kill me for saying this—sorry, poor choice of words, I guess. But she and Kristi were not getting on. Things were heading for a breakup. And it was going to be ugly. In a way, her passing is a good thing. We can sort this out with Leonard without too much problem, I hope, and everyone goes their own way."

"Someone told me the rumor was Kristi was getting Gary to raise the rent on the place to try to force Carol out," Martin said, watching Lyle intently.

Lyle exhaled loudly and shook his head. "I told her this would get out. No sense in hiding it. Yeah, that was the least of what she was doing. I just kept telling Carol to let go—there was no winning for anyone in keeping fighting. But she wouldn't."

"Why did Carol call you over last night?"

Lyle looked at Martin, his expression bleak. "She didn't. Kristi did."

It was Martin's turn to stare, while Lyle refused to meet his eyes. "Why did she call you?"

"I swear to God, Carol had nothing to do with killing Kristi," Lyle said. "I doubt she even knows how to load a gun, let alone shoot it."

"Why did Kristi call you?" Martin said, keeping his voice even.

Lyle sighed. "She wanted me to come and get Carol. She said Carol was threatening her."

"Threatening her how?"

"Threatening to kill her, I guess. I don't know. Kristi

didn't sound scared. She just wanted me to get Carol out of there."

Martin resisted the urge to shake his head. "And what time was this?"

"Ten or so, just like we said before." Lyle shook his head mournfully. "Look, I know how this looks and I know we should have come clean before, but Carol...she's scared, you understand. And she feels guilty, because her friend is dead and their last words together weren't so nice. And...you know."

Martin didn't, but he nodded. "What happened when you got to the Tea House?"

"Kristi was there, and Gary too. They both lit into me about Carol." He hesitated a moment. "I don't mind saying that I lit into them too."

"Where was Carol?" Martin said.

Why, he wondered, had Carol tried to cast the blame on Tyler and not Gary? Perhaps she'd hoped that Tyler wouldn't remember, but how could she know that Gary wouldn't report his involvement? And why hadn't he? At the moment it looked like he was the last to see Kristi alive, and maybe that was reason enough. Martin didn't think so, though. He wondered if Gary had been present when Tyler had shown up.

Lyle bent down to test the chains again. "She'd left already. She was home when I got back."

"So you left Gary and Kristi at the Tea House?"

Lyle nodded. "We should get started on this, I guess. They'll be starting to wonder."

"You realize you've just made yourself a suspect," Martin said. "And you've ruined Carol's alibi. Who's to say she didn't come back after you left?"

Lyle shook his head. "She didn't. She wouldn't. Like I said, she wouldn't know which end of the gun to point. I get that I'm a suspect, but she's not. There's no way she could've done that. No way."

He turned his back on Martin and started walking

toward the tractor. Martin nodded to himself, realizing that he would have to talk to Carol about this as well. But that could wait for tomorrow, when he could hopefully get her alone, away from her husband. In the meantime, he still needed to speak with Kristi's brother and hope he didn't further complicate the already messy situation.

14

Kevin Mzikevitch answered the door with a slight smile and nod. "Still coming down," he said, glancing up at the night sky. As with all the Mzikevitch children he was lean and dark-haired and looked as though he'd just spent the afternoon in the sun.

Martin nodded. "I'm going to have a hell of a time getting back into town."

"Don't go back tonight," Laureen said, emerging from downstairs. She was a compact woman, with red hair that fell almost to her shoulders. Like her husband, she was in her late thirties, but could easily have passed for ten years younger. "That's too dangerous. You can spend the night here. We've got a bed here for you. The Special Areas should have the road plowed by then."

"If they can get the plows out," Kevin said with a smile.

"They may have trouble," Martin said with a shake of his head. "I may take you up on your offer. It was damned stupid of me to head out tonight."

Laureen conducted them into the kitchen once Martin had his coat and boots off, and they sat around the table. Kevin offered him a drink, which sorely tempted Martin, but he forced himself to decline. Kevin poured himself a belt of rye and sat down. An awkward silence descended, which Martin let grow as he pulled out his notebook and pen and adjusted himself in his seat.

"I understand that you and your sister had a difficult relationship," Martin said. "Would you mind telling me about that?"

"I don't see how that's relevant," Laureen said in a sharp voice. Her dark eyes flashed with anger.

"Everything is relevant," Martin said with a shrug. He adjusted himself in his seat. His chair was one of those large, padded-leather things with wheels that gave the appearance of comfort without actually providing any. "I have to pursue any lead until I can exclude it. You told me on the phone you hadn't spoken in five years. Obviously something went bad. That, unfortunately, makes you a suspect."

"Well, I was here all yesterday and last night. Laureen can tell you that much," Kevin said.

Laureen nodded. "That's right. Neither of us left the farm yesterday.

"I understand," Martin said. "I'd still like to hear about it, though. It might help me to better understand what's been going on with Kristi these last few days and months. Put it in perspective, you understand. The picture you are painting is a lot different than the one she presented."

Kevin grimaced. "She took after my father the most, I would say. She and Karen, really. Maybe that's why they didn't get on well. Anyway, she never really forgave him for not giving her any part of the ranch. When Dad passed and she couldn't fight with him about it, she fought with me. It got personal with her and Laureen. It always gets personal with family."

He shrugged and took a drink. "Anyway, like I said, we stopped talking about five years ago."

"She doesn't even say hello when we pass her in the street," Laureen said.

"When was the last time you saw her?"

Kevin thought for a moment. "Two days ago. I had to go into the Hardy's for parts."

"And she wasn't any different than before."

"No, no. All the same. We've been doing a bit of business between our lawyers over the ranch and Dad's will, but that's been ongoing. The last time we met over that was a month ago."

"And there was no change there?"

Kevin hesitated a moment. "Nope. Just the same as always. Dragging things along. You know how lawyers are."

"This still about your father's estate? He's been gone for a while now, hasn't he?"

"Six years," Kevin said with a shake of his head. "He left a mess for us, that's for sure. Stipulations and whatnot. Seems like he set it up so that no one could get what they wanted out of it. Hell of a thing. That's what drove the final wedge between the three of us. I don't know if there's any way to put it back together. Not now, I guess."

"It was all settled till a year ago," Laureen said. "And then Kristi and Karen got together and decided to unsettle everything. Dragged us right back down into this hell."

Her voice was brittle with emotion. Martin nodded sympathetically. "How did Kristi and Karen get on?"

"Kristi didn't get on with anyone, unless she was getting something from them," Laureen said.

Kevin winced and shrugged. "Like I said. Things got personal. Money and family don't always mix. All three of us were pretty much at odds after Dad died. I don't know how Kristi got Karen back onside. I know Karen would never trust her. She's too smart for that."

Martin resisted a sigh and quelled the urge to ask for a drink. "I'm going to need specifics here. I know how difficult it is going into this stuff, but it could impact the investigation."

Kevin frowned and pursed his lips, either unsure or

unwilling to say any more. It was Laureen who spoke. "Oh for God's sake, let's get this into the open. Haven't you three suffered enough from what your father did? Your sister may have been killed for it."

"People think they know, but they don't know the whole of it," Kevin said. "And I'd rather they didn't. Dad was respected in this community. He doesn't need to have his name dragged through the mud like ours have been."

He paused, and Martin didn't reply. There was no telling him he could keep it a secret, not if it impacted the case. It would all come out in court then. Kevin nodded as if he understood, and continued.

"Dad gave me all the land in his last will. That had been agreed to before he died, although Karen and Kristi will tell you different. He wanted his name to carry on on the land, you understand. Anyway, whatever the reason, he gave it all to me. Or what he could. Some of it had all three of us and him listed as owners. The section with the old home quarter on it. He put a clause in the will that Karen and Kristi had to sign it over to me for them to get their inheritance.

"Some bonds and the insurance policy and all that," he said in answer to Martin's unasked question. "So anyway, we couldn't come to an agreement after Dad died. There's oil on that section, and so they didn't feel they were getting full value for it for giving up their right to it. For a while it looked like the lawyers were going to get it all, but we came to an agreement. Or at least I thought we had."

"We had," Laureen said firmly. "We had."

"What was the settlement?" Martin said.

"Well, I got the land and they got some more money from me to buy them out. And then they got their part of the estate. The problem came this year when Kristi decided she hadn't gotten proper value for the land because of the oil on it—there's about ten wells on it now, I guess—and so she convinced Karen they should take me to court over it. Say that I misrepresented things and that they should be getting a cut of the oil royalties. It was a mess."

"Did they have a case?"

"You know how lawyers are." Kevin shrugged. "They can make a case out of anything. I mean, they were talking about going back and contesting the whole will because they didn't think Dad was in his right mind when he signed it."

"And that's where things stand now?" Martin said, looking from Kevin to Laureen.

"I guess so, though who knows what Karen will do now. Not like they need the money. Not like Kristi did either, really, but she was the one who pushed Karen into it, I think."

"That's just what she did to everyone," Laureen said in a disapproving tone.

Kevin looked as though he was going to dispute what she said, but he fell silent and shrugged. "Hell of a mess in all, hell of mess."

Martin did not reply, but he had to agree, and somehow he had to untangle all these disparate threads and find some sort of truth in them. One of them led to Kristi's killer, but he had no idea which one. At the moment it seemed an impossible task.

Martin stayed at the kitchen table a little longer chatting with Kevin and Laureen about this and that. They were curious about his previous postings in Wetaskawin and Prince Albert, and how they compared to this one. He stayed as long as he felt was polite and then excused himself and said he needed to go to bed. Laureen showed him to his room.

It was in the basement, which stood in stark contrast to the rest of the house. Upstairs nothing had seemed out of place, and the dark wood of floor shone brightly, announcing its spotlessness. Here was all the detritus that was excluded above. Exercise machines and a random assortment of mismatched chairs. In one corner there was a turquoise couch set in front of a television perched on a VCR.

There were mats thrown over the floor, hiding concrete, and the ceiling was a warren of exposed pipes and wires. The bedroom, which was tucked into the far corner, had no door, and gave Martin the sense of a project given up on.

"You'll be up when Kevin gets up," she said apologetically, gesturing at the unfinished walls and ceiling. "You hear everything in the kitchen down here."

"That's fine," he said. "I need to be getting an early start on the day anyway."

When she left him, he sat in a chair by the bedside and went over his notes from the day. All this work and he felt no closer to a solution than he had when he first looked upon Kristi's body this morning. It didn't feel possible that only a day had passed. His head ached and he wanted a cigarette. He briefly found himself wondering if Kevin or Laureen smoked, but forced himself to look at his notes again.

Although he now knew where Kristi had been killed, it had not limited his suspects in any way. Tyler was still at the forefront of his mind, despite everything else he had discovered. He could easily have come back to the Tea House after Kristi had sent him away, especially if he happened to see Gary there. For that matter, Gary was also a suspect, and Martin's first stop tomorrow would be to talk with him about what he had been doing there that night.

If Lyle was to be believed, and Martin did not doubt his sincerity, then Carol could be eliminated as a suspect, but he could not. Nor could Karen, with Arnold absent at the bar while the murder took place. She had grown up on a farm, so she would know how to fire a shotgun. Kevin and Laureen had each other as alibis, but he did not trust them entirely. Not when so many others had spent the day lying to him. Their hatred of Kristi was too obvious, as was their motive.

Was that all? No, he realized. He could not exclude Leonard yet either. Could he have slipped away while Clarissa was in her room chatting with her friends and listening to music? Unlikely, but Martin could not entirely dismiss the possibility.

All of these people would have had easy access to a shotgun, and all of them could have found themselves at the Tea House after Carol left. But which of them had reason enough to want Kristi dead?

That was a question for tomorrow, he realized, feeling the full weight of exhaustion settle upon him. It had been a long and stressful day, and he had only just begun. Tomorrow would be more of the same. He could only hope that someone from the Youngstown or Hanna detachments would be able to join him. Perhaps the forensics team from Calgary as well. There was too much to do for just one person, and he still could not escape the feeling that he was missing something vital.

He got undressed and went to bed, falling asleep almost as soon as he lay down. His dreams were of vast pastures filled with rolling hills, endless horizons, all covered in snow, which continued to descend, covering everything until only darkness remained.

15

There was light coming through the narrow window above his head when Martin awoke the next morning. The floors above him creaked with footsteps, and he fumbled for his watch, only to discover that it was already past eight. He swore to himself. Far too late to be starting on this day with so much to do. He hurried into his clothes and went upstairs.

Laureen was in kitchen, as well as her two sons, eight and ten, who stared at him wide-eyed as he entered.

"How did you sleep, Martin?" Laureen said, glancing at him from the counter where she was whipping some eggs.

"Too well," he said, sleep still heavy in his voice. "I was hoping to be back in Loverna by now."

"Oh, I know. Sorry. Kevin wanted to wake you, but I said to let you sleep. You just looked so tired last night, I thought you could use it. The plow just went by about ten minutes ago, though, so you should be able to get back to town quick."

"That's good," Martin said, sitting down at the table and smiling at the two boys. "School's still closed, I take it?"

"Yeah, not many roads plowed yet. Can I get you some

coffee? How about something to eat? I'm making the boys scrambled eggs. I can easily make some for you."

Martin told her that would be fine, and helped himself to some coffee, digging the milk out of the fridge. As he ate his breakfast, chatting with Laureen and the two boys, he planned out his day. First, he thought, with the plow going by, he should make a stop at the Hutterite colony and solve at least one mystery for the day. After that he would head back into town and have a chat with Gary and Karen, test their stories. From there, he wasn't sure. Hopefully by then some help would have arrived.

He finished breakfast quickly, not lingering to chat with Laureen, and made his way to his car. As he was getting in, Kevin drove by in a truck with a dead calf hanging out the back end. Seeing Martin, he pulled to a stop and got out.

"Heading back to town, then?"

"Yes," Martin said. "Back to work. Thanks for your help last night, and the bed."

"Not a problem at all. Let me know if there's anything else you need. Laureen and I are happy to help. Whatever our differences with Kristi, no one deserves that. No one."

Martin nodded his thanks and gestured at the dead calf. "Looks like a tough morning."

Kevin scowled and shook his head. "Worst time of year for a storm like this. Bet we lost fifteen calves yesterday. Cows had them and they froze in the snow, and there was no way I could even get out to them. Just lucky we didn't have more."

"It's a hell of a lot of snow," Martin said.

"That it is," Kevin said, and, with a wave, turned and headed back for his truck. Martin got in his car and pulled out onto the highway, which, as Laureen had promised, was freshly plowed. Seeing it made him oddly hopeful, and he turned west, heading away from town and toward the Hutterite colony.

The Loverna Hutterite Colony was one of nearly two

hundred such communes in the province. The Hutterites, like their distant cousins the Amish, were a religious sect originally from Germany who had come to Canada to escape persecution. Unlike the Amish, the Hutterites used modern technology in their farming methods, but they banned televisions and the internet and things of that nature.

The communes all looked much the same to Martin, vast complexes with pig and chicken barns, cattle pens, and nearly a quarter section set aside for the gardens. The houses were all the same: single storied and interlocking. There was a school that children attended, by agreement with the provincial government, until they were sixteen years old, and a large hall where meals were taken.

Martin had been told, though he had no idea if it were true, that the men ate first, then the children, and finally the women, who were left to clean everything. Lara, in fact, had told him that, bristling at what she perceived as their subjugation. If it was a rumor, it was one of the kinder ones he had heard about the colony and Hutterites in general.

They existed uneasily within the larger Loverna community, their constant attempts to expand their operations delighting those whose land prices they drove up, while worrying others who saw something untoward in it all. There were those who claimed that Hutterites were nothing but thieves and drunks and worse, but in Martin's few interactions with them they had proven themselves to be polite and unassuming, wanting only to be left to their ways.

As he pulled into the yard, he saw several men, wearing their standard dress of black and white, all of it unchanged in style from the nineteenth century. The men all waved at Martin as he came to a stop, one of them stepping away from the group to come over to talk with him.

"What can I do for you, Martin?" he said in his thick German accent.

"Hello, Sam," Martin said. "You folks doing all right after the storm?"

"Sure, sure," Sam said with a nod. Martin guessed he was about sixty, with a carefully trimmed beard that had gone grey and was slowly turning white. "We're used to this by now."

"I suppose you are."

"You just checking in on us? I figured you would be busy with that business over at Johnstone's. Terrible, terrible."

One day and even the Hutterites had heard, in the midst of the worst spring snowstorm in decades. Everyone knew, that much was evident. Did that matter? Likely not, Martin decided.

"That's what I'm here about, actually," he said.

The Hutterite's shock could not have been more obvious. Martin had never seen so undisguised a double take. "Surely you don't think someone here—"

"No," Martin said quickly. "Nothing I've seen leads me to believe that. But I do have some concerns. After we removed the body, someone walked over the crime scene and down into the coulee. I'm just trying to determine whether that was an honest mistake or if someone was there trying to hide evidence."

"And you think someone here did it?"

Martin nodded, watching the Hutterite closely. "Someone had come across Leonard's pasture, across the highway and down into the coulee."

"Why would you think someone here would do that?" Sam said, shaking his head.

"Well, I remember last winter when some of your boys here had a trapline set up in Wayne's coulee. Illegally, I might add. Now, as disappointed as I would be if that's the case again, it would also set my mind at ease as to know that's all it was."

Sam pursed his lips and looked as if he were about to argue some more, but then he nodded and said in a quiet voice, "I'll ask the boys and we'll see. I'll let you know."

Martin nodded his thanks and got back in his car. That was all the confirmation he needed. As he started onto the highway, he got out his phone and called Harold Winship, the local Fish and Wildlife officer, to let him know that he suspected the Hutterites were running another illegal trapline. They would have to wait to deal with it until after he had finished with Kristi's murder. Hopefully when the effects of the storm were not so evident.

The weight on his chest did not feel so heavy now with one mystery solved and the highway clear before him. He turned on the radio as he drove back into town, whistling along to the tune.

16

His first stop was out at the gas bar to see Gary, but only Tammy was present, staring wanly out at the parking lot from her station behind the counter. He was about to head back to his car and return to town when impulse made him stop and look at her more closely.

"You heard about Kristi Taid, I imagine?" he said.

"Awful," Tammy said in a quiet voice.

"What do you know about Kristi and Gary?" He said it in an offhand way that implied something while saying nothing.

Tammy flushed red and shook her head. "Nothing," she said. "I don't know nothing about that."

"But they had to work together a bit, didn't they?" he said, playing the innocent. "I mean, Kristi and Carol were leasing the Tea House building from him."

"I guess," she said, her voice heavy with emotion. "I guess."

"I could have you arrested for impeding an investigation into a murder," Martin said, deciding to see if a little pressure would help hasten the process. "Now, what can you tell me about Gary and Kristi?"

Tammy looked as though she were about to burst into

tears. "They had some deal going on. I don't know exactly. He wouldn't really talk about it with me."

"Is that all?" he said, hating himself for doing this.

She shook her head. "No. They were together."

Tears did begin to flow then, and he waited for her to regain control. "Sorry," she said as she took a tissue and blew her nose.

"It's not a problem," he said. "You two were together as well, I take it."

She gave a kind of half-nod and would not meet his eyes. When, Martin wondered, had that begun? She was only eighteen years old. He felt a slow burn of anger course through him at the confirmation of his suspicions that Gary was slime. It felt good in a way, though there was nothing illegal in what Gary had done. Consent was sixteen. Still made him an asshole.

"When did you find out?" he said.

"Yesterday," she said, beginning to cry again. "He told me he needed me to say that we were together last night. When I asked him why, he said that he was with Kristi right before she died and he needed an alibi. And when I asked him why they were together, he wouldn't say, but…he told me he loved me."

The last was said with fury that almost made Martin smile. "But you wouldn't be his alibi?"

"Hell no," Tammy said. "Hell no. That bastard can make his own alibi. I bet he'll try with his wife next."

"I imagine he will," Martin said.

"That's why I phoned her this morning, to let her know that he'd already tried the same thing with me. Cuz I know he'll be giving her some song and dance like he gave me."

Martin nodded, careful not to show what he was thinking. Tammy had just set off a bomb, and he was curious to see how far the shrapnel would spread.

"What did Roxanne say?"

"She just thanked me for letting her know," Tammy

said with a small smile.

"Now maybe you can take me through what happened the day before," Martin said. "You were working, right?"

"From noon till we closed at nine."

"What time did Gary leave?"

"He went home for supper and then came back around eight because he had to arrange for a delivery first thing in the morning."

"What delivery was that?" Martin said, going to fix himself a cup of coffee.

Tammy shrugged. "I don't know the schedule. He never told me that stuff. Him or Richard or Russell would know."

"You were here first thing yesterday. Did one of them come by with the truck?" Martin said.

"Nope. Probably cuz of the storm, though, right?"

"Probably," Martin said, though he wondered if that was actually the case. There was the matter of the stolen gas, of course. "When did Gary leave that night?"

"Oh, not long after, actually. He was only here ten minutes or so. Said he wanted to catch up with Richard at the bar before he got too far in."

He took a sip of the coffee he had poured and winced as it stung his mouth with its heat. "Did he say why he was going to meet Richard?"

Tammy shook her head.

"And what about yesterday? You were here first thing. What time did he get in?"

She thought for a moment. "Not until close to nine, I guess. That's late for him. He went out and checked the tanks—he does that all the time now since the thefts started—and came back and called you."

"Did he seem different to you?" he said, and tried the coffee again.

"He was mad as hell, but I just figured he and Roxanne had a fight and that's why he was late."

A trucker, stranded no doubt by the storm, came into

the store to buy a chocolate bar, and Martin waited until he paid and left before continuing with Tammy.

"Was he normally mad about the gas being stolen?"

"No, it didn't seem like he really cared, to be honest," Tammy said. "I thought it was weird, actually."

It was strange, Martin thought, unless Gary was involved in the thefts, which was beginning to seem more and more of a possibility. "And when did he ask you to be his alibi?"

"Not till last night," Tammy said. "He stopped by my place to… We really had it out for a while."

"Do you remember what time?" he said, trying not to show how important her answer was.

"It was late, you know. Nine, I guess."

Martin thanked her and went out to his car, trying not to rush, though he desperately wanted to. It was evident now that Gary was at the center of this whole mess, and Martin needed to talk to him as soon as possible. The urgency he felt was ridiculous, he told himself. Gary wasn't going anywhere. To do so now would only cast more suspicion on himself.

Before he could start back for town, dispatch got hold of him on the radio. Someone would be coming from Hanna as soon as the highways were deemed safe and reopened. Apparently they still had not been between Hanna and Youngstown. They hoped to be here by late in the afternoon, the dispatcher told him. The forensics team had left Calgary that morning, but they would be stopped at Hanna as well, assuming they managed to make it that far today.

That was an open question as well. There was a chance of more snow, according to the radio. A second storm was coming down from the mountains and across the province, which would only further complicate matters. It all did not look good for support arriving today. Someone would come eventually to help him, Martin reassured himself, and in the meantime, none of his suspects would be straying too far. Which meant there was work to be done.

It was Roxanne Seedstrom who answered the door when he rang the doorbell. She did not look surprised to see him, her expression grim and knowing, her smile curt. Martin could hear a young child wailing behind her, which she seemed oblivious to.

"He's not here," she said. As always, Martin was surprised at her youth, though he couldn't say why. She was, he guessed, in her mid-twenties and very attractive. The thought of her being married to Gary always left Martin both baffled and annoyed, though what it mattered to him he could not say.

Martin nodded. "May I come in? I have some questions for you as well."

She gave half a shrug and turned around, leaving him in the doorway, to quiet the child who was crying. Martin closed the door, took off his boots, and made his way into the kitchen, where Roxanne was soothing a girl, no more than two, her face still glistening with tears. At her feet was a young, golden-haired boy, with Gary's impish features, who stared up at Martin with wide eyes.

"We've had a difficult morning, haven't we?" Roxanne whispered to the girl as she bounced her in her arms.

"Do you know where Gary is?" Martin said in a low voice, though he couldn't say why he was being quiet. The children would both be able to hear what he was saying.

"At the motel, I imagine, unless he's gone to try to patch things up with that little slut of his."

"I was just talking with her," Martin said, though he wasn't sure why he was telling Roxanne this. "Gary wasn't there."

"Is that supposed to make me feel better?"

"No," Martin said, refusing to say any more.

"Goddamn him. Goddamn him. We've got two kids and he's fucking around with that child. She's only eighteen. God knows when it started. It just makes me sick. How could he do that to her?"

Roxanne was so angry her cheeks were flushed red and the arms that held her daughter were trembling. The girl looked scared and Martin could not blame her. He noticed that Roxanne's hair, long and with precise waving curls that could only come from a salon, did not have a strand out of place.

"And then to have to hear it from her. My God, everyone probably knew but me, didn't they? My God. How could he? I feel like such a fool."

Martin nodded reflexively, waiting for her to say her piece. "Did he ask you to be an alibi for him for the night Kristi Taid was killed?"

"No," she said, practically vibrating with anger. "No. The first I heard of it was when she phoned. Was he fucking her too?"

"I have no idea," Martin said. "But he was one of the last people to see her alive, best I can tell. Can you tell me what he was doing that night?"

"I just can't believe any of this," Roxanne said, sitting down at the kitchen table, still clutching the young girl, who had begun to squirm in her arms. She set her down, and the girl rejoined her brother on the floor, the two of them playing with the toys that were scattered there.

"It's very important that you tell me everything that happened that night. Anything that you can remember," Martin said, taking the opportunity to sit across from her.

Roxanne nodded distractedly. "He was home for supper, like usual. Then he said he had to go to the office to get some paperwork done for a delivery. After that he was going to stop by with the boys for a quick drink. I didn't think anything of it. He's done it so often. God, I'm such an idiot. He was fucking her every time, wasn't he?"

"I'm trying to determine what he was doing that night," Martin said gently. "Now, what time did he get back?"

"It was late. I'd already gone to bed. I woke up when

he got into bed. It was around one, I would guess. Maybe earlier, maybe later. I wasn't really awake, you know. I just remember he was freezing."

"He said that to you?"

"No, I rolled over to…" She shook her head, tears welling in her eyes. "His hands were like ice."

"And that was unusual for him?" Martin said.

"Not if he'd been outside for a while," Roxanne said, stating the obvious.

"Did he say anything that night?"

Roxanne shook her head. "If he did, I don't remember. I fell back asleep right away."

"Okay," Martin said. "How about the next morning? Did he seem different? Anything unusual happen?"

"No, he seemed himself. He went to work first thing. He came back for lunch and mentioned that he'd heard Kristi Taid had been killed, but he said he didn't know anything about it. That was it, really. You don't think he did it, do you?"

"Like I said, he was one of the last people to see Kristi alive, based on what I've heard from others. He was at the Tea House the night she was killed, but I don't know what for. He didn't mention anything about going there, did he? Or about the lease?"

Roxanne thought for a moment. "No, I don't think so. He'd mentioned a while ago he was thinking about raising the rent when the lease expired, but I didn't think it was anything serious. I doubt they can afford much more than they're paying right now."

Martin stood up from the table, as the elder child asked Roxanne a question. "If you think of anything else, please let me know. Like I said, it could be very important. I'm just trying to establish a timeline of Kristi's final night, and the more detail I have, the better. And if Gary comes back here or calls you, let him know to get in touch with me."

Roxanne said she would, and Martin went to the front of the house to put on his boots while she answered the boy's question. Martin called out a goodbye and went out the door without waiting for a response. Outside he saw it had begun to snow again, wet flakes filling the air.

17

There were two places in town where Gary might be staying while hoping that Roxanne would cool off and let him come crawling back. Martin did not like his odds there—Roxanne was feistier than he had expected—though by now he should be used to the fact that his initial impressions of everyone in the town had only led him astray. Except for Gary, apparently, whom Martin had always suspected of being a bastard of the highest order. His mistake had been in thinking that he was ultimately harmless, which, as was becoming more and more evident, was not the case at all.

Martin drove to the nearest option, the Deerfoot Motel, just off First Avenue near the entrance to town. The other possibility was the new hotel out on the highway near the gas bar, but he suspected Gary would also want to stay clear of Tammy for the next little while. The Hotel was not a possibility, not for someone with Gary's means. The rooms there, Martin felt very certain, should not be let out, though he knew they were. The building was up to code for the 1930s, but otherwise it was not suitable for habitation unless someone was broke and desperate.

Marshall Beauregard, the owner of the Deerfoot, was at the front desk when Martin walked into lobby of the motel. "How can I help you, constable?" he said, glancing up from the crossword he was completing.

"I'm looking for Gary Seedstrom," Martin said, leaning against the counter. "Roxanne said he might have checked in here."

Marshall gave a knowing little nod to Martin. "He sure did. Room 209. As far as I know he's still in there, but it's around back, so he could have taken off. Do you want me to call?"

"That's all right. I'll just head around back. Thanks," Martin said, turning to go. Marshall did not reply, returning to his crossword.

Martin walked around to the other side of the motel, not bothering to move his car. The snow was not coming as thick as yesterday, but it was steady, and it would not be long before they would need to start plowing the roads again. If it was snowing here it had probably been snowing in the west for an hour or more, which meant that the road between Hanna and Youngstown might never have opened.

He couldn't have said why that worry continued to burrow into his thoughts. His way forward now was clear. Gary was his main suspect. He had only to talk to him and perhaps Karen as well, the better to exclude her from involvement. Once the storm passed the forensics team would see to the evidence he needed.

Now that he felt on the precipice of making an arrest, each step he took began to feel as though it mattered more. Every decision he made, every question he asked, could impact whether he could make a case against the killer. That had been the case from the beginning, but he felt it now more than at any point, except for those moments when he had first laid eyes upon Kristi Taid's body.

If Lara were here... But he forced that thought aside.

She was not, nor was anyone from Youngstown or Hanna, nor was the forensics team. He was going to have to do this alone.

He came to room 209 and knocked on the door. There was no response, and he knocked again, calling out this time as well. "Gary, it's Constable Thomas. I just have a few questions for you."

Martin put his ear to the door and was met with silence within. He considered his options and decided to leave questioning Gary aside for the time being. The man wasn't going anywhere, not with the snow continuing to fall, and Martin's time was better spent following other leads than chasing Gary around town. Loverna was small, and he would be found eventually.

He went back around to the front and told Marshall to keep an eye out for Gary and to have him call if he came by. Marshall solemnly promised he would before returning to his crossword. Satisfied that he had done all he could there, Martin drove over to the Mahls' house to talk with Karen.

"Christ, still coming down, is it?" Arnold said as he opened the door and waved Martin in.

"I expect you'll be wanting to chat with Karen," he added in a low voice. "She's with someone right now. But you're welcome to wait."

Martin nodded. "Who's here?"

"Helen," Arnold said, unable to stop himself from making a face.

Martin smiled. "I see. Well, I have a few questions for you as well, if you don't mind while we wait."

"Interrogate away. We may have the whole afternoon ahead of us."

"So, Karen tells me you were at the Hotel that night. What time did you get there and what time did you leave?"

"Yeah, Ted and I always go there after the school board meetings. Kristi was there at the meeting, but I'm sure you already know that. Anyway, I guess we got there around nine. And it was after midnight when I got back, which did not put me in the good books, let me tell you."

"I can imagine," Martin said. They remained standing in the entryway. In the kitchen he could just hear Helen saying something, though he could not make out any of the words. "Who else was at the Hotel that night?"

"Most of the usual suspects, I guess. Cory and Russell, Richard and Ty. They were carrying on loud as anything. Blaine and Annalise were there too." Arnold paused to consider who else.

"You happen to see Gary stop by?"

Arnold shook his head.

"Do you remember what time those four boys left?"

"Oh, they were all still there when I left," Arnold said. "No, that's not right. Ty had gone. And Richard too for a bit. But I'm not sure when they left exactly."

Martin nodded. Everything checked out with what others had told him, more or less. It still left Gary unaccounted for between eight and ten on the night in question. He was the linchpin in so many ways. If Lyle was to be believed, and Martin tended to think so, then Gary was the last to see Kristi alive. Gary either had killed her himself, though Martin could find no motive for his doing so, or he knew where she had gone and who might have.

Arnold gave an involuntary shrug. "That all you got for me, then? Let me go see if I can hurry Helen along. Send help if I don't come back."

Arnold turned and headed into the kitchen while Martin took off his boots and coat. He lingered in the hallway by the entrance, studying the pictures hanging on the wall. There were pictures of Arnold and Karen's three kids, all grown up and left home now, as well as of Arnold's extended family, his parents and aunts and cousins. Karen's extended family was absent from the wall, but for one picture of the parents with the three children, taken in happier days when all three were still in the bloom of youth. Something had gone terribly wrong in the intervening years, or perhaps the rot had begun here, left unseen until the patriarch had left them to squabble over the spoils of the throne.

When he tired of contemplating the pictures and building unprovable theories from them, Martin made his way to the kitchen, where Helen and Karen sat across from each other at the table, while Arnold hovered uncomfortably by one of the counters. Everyone looked up at Martin's entrance, and he smiled.

"I'm sorry, Helen, but you'll have to excuse me. I've got a few questions for Karen that I need to ask her now."

"Oh, oh," Helen said, looking wildly around the room from face to face, unsure what to do. "I'm sorry. I didn't realize."

"Not to worry," Martin said with a smile. "Not to worry. I hate to interrupt, but I'm pressed for time."

Helen still seemed at a loss as to how to react, and looked to Karen for help. Karen stood up from her chair and turned to Arnold. "I'd be happy to answer your questions, Martin. Arnold, why don't you show Helen to the door?"

Arnold leapt up from the counter, took Helen by the arm, and led her out of the kitchen, while Karen turned to Martin and rolled her eyes.

"It's been a busy couple of days for you, I imagine," Karen said in a low voice. "Have you found out anything about what happened to Kristi?"

"I've found out a number of things," Martin said, gesturing for her to sit. He took Helen's chair opposite her. "That's why I'm back here now."

Karen nodded, a frown pinching her face. "You've been talking to Kevin, I guess."

Martin nodded in turn, not saying anything. They could both hear Helen loudly saying goodbye to Arnold, followed by the door slamming shut. Arnold stuck his head into the kitchen.

"She's gone," he said, with a smile. "I'll just head out and shovel the walk, hon. Give you guys some space."

Martin smiled his thanks at Arnold. Karen sighed and shook her head, looking away from him. "I should have told you, I know, but I was hoping you would find somebody before… It's embarrassing, frankly, this whole thing with our family. We shouldn't be like this, but we are."

"So what were you like?"

Karen closed her eyes, visibly collecting herself, and then began to speak. "Kristi came to me earlier this year saying that, according to the terms of the will, we hadn't been properly compensated. I suppose Kevin told you about Dad's will. Or at least his version of it. Well, according to the terms, we had to sell Kevin the old home quarter to get the rest of our inheritance, which was a pittance, really. Anyway, Kevin was supposed to pay us fair market value for our share in order for him to get the land that was still in Dad's name.

"As you can imagine, we went back and forth over what fair market value was. The problem is that it's most valuable to Kevin, because he uses it for his corrals and bins and storage. No one else would use it for anything but pasture land. Mom and Dad's house is still there, but no one could live in it now without major work being done. So it doesn't have the value a farm site normally would, if you understand."

Karen halted and held out her hands, as though to stop herself from going on. "None of that's here or there, I guess. The point is, we fought about it, the lawyers were involved, and eventually we settled on something. I don't suppose anyone was all that happy. Last fall Kristi came to me and said that she thought we hadn't gotten fair market value, because they found oil on the land. She thought that Kevin had known about the oil and hadn't told us. She wanted to take him to court and contest the will."

"And you agreed?" Martin said.

"Against my better judgment," she said. "But yes, I did. Kevin has always been so…acting like the farm was his birthright. It was all our birthrights. We all put our time in there with Dad, and he gets to have all the reward for surviving that. It was stupid, though—no matter what, even if we had won, the lawyers would probably have taken it all. Kevin would have made sure of that. So I told Kristi that I was going to drop the claim."

"When did you do that?" Martin said.

"That morning, when she stopped by for coffee."

"How did she react?"

"Oh, she was furious, of course. How could she not be? I think she was maybe counting on it, you know. I've heard the Tea House wasn't doing as well as they would've liked, and she was unhappy with Carol, so she wanted to get out from that. The extra money would have been a big help."

She still had not met his eyes, Martin noted, but what she said made sense. Kristi may or may not have needed the money, but given her dealings with Carol and Gary, she obviously had no qualms about taking what she felt was owed her. One thing he could be certain of: the Mahls had no need of money, to judge by this house.

"Do you think Kevin could have killed Kristi? Just to stop the court case?" Martin said, watching to see her reaction.

"Oh no, no," she said very firmly. "Laureen wouldn't let him do something like that. That's unfair, but it's true. Anyway, he didn't know I was dropping the case, so what good would killing her do? For all he knew, I would still pursue it."

"Is there anything else you can think of? Anything else you'd like to add about that night?" Martin said.

Karen's eyes narrowed. "I've told you nothing but the truth here. Nothing but the truth. And I have nothing to add to it. If you suspect me of anything, you just let me know."

Martin did not point out that she had withheld information about the ongoing dispute with Kevin and the rest of their family history. He suspected he had not heard all of it, but for all he knew, she might be correct and it might have no bearing on the matter at hand. He was not sure, though, and he wouldn't be until he talked to Gary.

He smiled at Karen. "This is still an open investigation, so I need to ask questions that make people a little uncomfortable. If there's anything else you're not telling me now, anything else you can think of, even if you don't think it's relevant, I'd appreciate you letting me know."

Karen flinched a bit at his words but did not reply. Martin got up from the table and let himself out, Karen not stirring at all from where she sat, staring off into the distance. He was not sure what to make of that, but he did not have time to dwell on it. There was the more pressing matter of Gary's whereabouts.

Outside it was still snowing, and Arnold was leaning on his shovel chatting with Peggy Mirtle. There was already an inch or so of snow on the sidewalks where Arnold hadn't shoveled. Martin waved to the two of them and got in his car, heading back for the Deerfoot Motel to confront Gary.

18

Martin returned to the motel, this time heading straight around to the back, where Gary's room was. There was no answer when he knocked on the door. He was about to knock again when he spotted a snow-covered truck at the far end of the parking lot. He walked over to it and brushed some of the snow off its hood. It was Gary's, he was certain, though he called in to dispatch to be sure.

There was, he estimated, over an inch of snow on the truck, so it had to have been there at least since he had been here before, if not earlier. Had it been there when he had first come looking for Gary? He racked his brain but could not recall. A pit seemed to have opened in his stomach, and he felt ill, sweat beading on his forehead and back in spite of the chill in the air.

He had dispatch pull up Gary's cell number, and he dialed it while standing outside the motel room, his ear pressed against the door. His heart was echoing in his ear, but still he could hear the abrasive squawk of the ringtone somewhere within. He pocketed his own phone and made his way around to front desk, where Marshall sat busy with another crossword.

"You seen Gary at all?" Martin said, trying to keep his

voice steady and nonchalant.

Marshall looked up from his puzzle. "Nope. Like I said, though, he could come and go and come and go again from that room and I wouldn't necessarily see a thing."

"Right," Martin said, nodding and looking out at the street. "What if something was going on in the room, an argument or something? Would you hear that?"

Marshall shook his head. "The walls are pretty good here, really. I can hear what's going on pretty well from the rooms immediately by the lobby here. But that one's pretty far away."

"I'm going to need you to open up Gary's room for me."

"Don't you need a warrant for that?" Marshall said, looking confused.

"This is an emergency. I just tried Gary's cell. It's in the room and he's not answering it."

"Maybe he forgot it."

"His truck's parked out back too," Martin said with a shake of his head. He was certain now what he would find within the room, could feel the inevitably of it. Somewhere he had missed something, been too slow to realize some fact, and Gary had paid the price.

"Okay," Marshall said reluctantly. "Let me get the key."

Martin watched impatiently as Marshall dug around his desk for his set of master keys and then struggled into his oversized winter parka. They walked around back, their feet crunching on the snow, to room 209. Marshall knocked on the door, calling out Gary's name, and, when he received no response, fumbled with his keys and unlocked the door. He stepped aside, looking away from the building out at the alley, letting Martin open the door.

He did, throwing it open and stepping onto the mat left at the entrance for boots. Gary's were set neatly off to the side. Martin found the light switch by the door and flicked it on, pushing back the shadows. There were some clothes on the bed and a suitcase thrown open. On a table by the window were a set of keys and a cell phone. Otherwise the room was empty.

By reflex he took his boots off, leaving them on the mat. He motioned for Marshall to stay out of the room, some instinct still telling him that things were terribly wrong here. Why were the lights out and the blinds closed, he wondered? Something about that bothered him. He looked around the room, stepping carefully, looking for any other signs that Gary was here or had left. But the boots, keys, and cell phone were proof enough—he was stalling for time, and he knew it.

At last he summoned the courage to go to the bathroom, which was at the far end of the room. The door hung partway open, obscuring most of what lay within. Martin reached out and pushed it gently. It swung back slowly, revealing Gary sitting naked on the toilet. His head was slumped into his chest at an odd angle, and Martin could see that his eyes were still open, staring blankly at the floor. His hands hung limp at his sides. There was blood on his chest, his legs, and a pool of it on the floor.

Martin swore under his breath, glancing back at Marshall, who remained hovering by the door, his hood flipped up against the cold. After debating for a moment, Martin dug into his jacket pocket, slipped on a plastic glove, and stepped into the bathroom. Being careful to avoid the pool of blood, he gingerly lifted up Gary's head, revealing the deep gash at his throat.

Martin took a look at the eyes, not bothering to check for a pulse, and studied the wound. It was deep, and looked to Martin as though it was the result of someone plunging a knife directly into the throat. A large blade, probably a hunting knife. There were no other wounds on the body, and a quick check of both his hands showed no signs of defensive wounds or a struggle of any kind. Gary had known his killer—and if his nakedness was any indication, possibly intimately.

The body was still warm, which meant Gary had been

killed while he was talking to Karen and Arnold, or before. The killer might even have still been in the room when Martin had first stopped by looking for Gary. He tried to recall the vehicles parked around the motel, if any of them belonged to anyone involved in Kristi's murder, but he didn't remember. He had not paid any attention to them.

This was where he needed Lara. Those were the sorts of details that never escaped her attention. "Dammit," he said, louder than he had intended.

"Everything all right there?" Marshall said, in a nervous voice.

"Stay there," Martin said, looking around the bathroom to see if there was anything else he might have missed. "This is a crime scene. Only police should enter. I'm going to need the keys from you."

There was no response from Marshall, but Martin didn't care. He was running his eyes over the floor around where Gary sat, the bathroom counter and sink, and finally the tub. Aside from some stray hairs in the sink, all of which could conceivably have come from Gary, to judge by the color, there was nothing of use that he could see. Not without forensics, anyway. Best to leave it all for them to look at when they got here.

He pulled the garbage out from under the sink counter, but it was more of the same. A few tissues and plastic wrappers from the complimentary soap and glasses. Forensics might be able to get something from it as well, but it would do little for him until they got here. He put it back under the sink and went over everything again, including Gary's body, to see if there was anything he had missed.

When he was satisfied there wasn't, he went back out into the main room. Marshall was still standing in the open doorway looking anxious. Martin went to him.

"Give me the keys to this room." Marshall handed them over automatically, and Martin pocketed them. "Are these the only ones?"

"The custodian has a pair too. What's happening? Is Gary all right?"

"No," Martin said. "He's not. When does the custodian normally come by?"

"First thing after lunch, normally."

"Make sure they know not to come in here. I'm going to be putting up police tape and everything, but I can't have anyone coming in here. Okay?"

"Right. Okay," Marshall said, nodding vigorously. "Is he...still in there?"

Martin hesitated. "Yes. No one's to come in here until the forensics team arrives. They're due in this afternoon. Maybe go phone the custodian now, just to be safe."

Marshall nodded, his lips moving oddly, and hurried back around to the front of the building, relief washing over his face as he went. Martin well understood that. He longed to follow behind the motel manager and leave this new body and all the problems that came with it to someone else. Instead he turned back to the room, shutting the door behind him.

He started with the clothes on the bed and saw that they were in the right combination to be the clothes Gary had been wearing that morning. Martin went through the pockets but found nothing of interest there. The suitcase had only clothes and other miscellanea that were irrelevant. The bureau drawers and closet were all empty, except for Gary's coat, which had only a comb and some toothpicks in it. The table had only his wallet, cell phone, and car keys, which Martin pocketed.

When Martin was done with his search he went over everything again a second time, just to be certain nothing had been missed. As he did so, something worked at the back of his mind, a niggling thought that was slowly transforming into a certainty. He was missing something. But what?

At last it dawned upon him as he turned to set up the police tape outside the room, and checked his pocket for the room key Marshall had given him. He had found no room key in amongst Gary's things. Whoever had killed him had taken it for some reason. Why would they have done that? Was it a mistake, or did they intend to come back for something?

He decided it had to be the former, given he had found nothing that seemed worth coming back for. It would be nice to be able to have someone to sit and watch the place just the same, to see if anyone of interest appeared. That was not a possibility now.

He slipped back into his boots and went outside. The snow was even heavier than before, and the wind had picked up and sent it swirling around the parking lot, stinging his eyes. Martin ignored it as best he could, setting the police tape in an X over the door before checking to make sure it was locked.

Before he put a call into dispatch to notify them of the murder, he went over Gary's truck, looking for anything that might be of relevance. The vehicle was immaculately clean and stank of air freshener. The truck's box held only snow. Anyone like Gary, who was carrying on multiple affairs, as well as whatever other schemes he was involved in, would take painstaking care to make sure no trace of anything could be found in so obvious a place as his truck, Martin supposed.

When he was satisfied there was nothing more to be found, he locked the truck and went to his car and called dispatch, notifying them of the murder and asking for an update on his backup. There was no change there, and he felt as though he had returned to the beginning with Gary's murder. He was no nearer to solving Kristi's death, and now the bodies were beginning to pile up.

19

As Martin sat in the car, struggling to piece together his thoughts, he found himself having difficulty breathing and had to force himself to take deep and steady breaths, keeping his eyes closed and his mind blank. When he had recovered, he made himself take a strict accounting of all the people who might be involved in this new death.

First, of course, was Roxanne—he would need to let her know what happened immediately, before anyone else did. Certainly she had been angry enough with Gary in the hours before his death. But he somehow doubted she would have left her kids alone to come here and kill him.

Tammy was a possibility as well, but had Gary told her where he was? Unlikely, and she had her shift at the UFA. If he wanted to have it out with her again, he would have gone there or to her place once her shift was done.

Though he had no evidence to suggest it, Martin felt quite certain that this death was connected with Kristi's in some way. It was the result of Gary's involvement with her—whatever that might have been—and the fact that he had been the last to see her alive. Possibly he could connect her killer to her as well, even if he hadn't been involved in the murder himself. That now seemed unlikely.

The connection was there; he just had to determine who it was connected them.

Karen was still a possibility. It would have been difficult but not impossible for her to kill Gary this morning and make it back before he and Helen came by. Martin made a note to ask Helen what time she got there. Was Karen strong enough to cause such a wound? She didn't appear to be, but he decided she likely was. She was a farm girl, after all, despite appearances now.

Lyle remained a suspect, of course. As did Carol, if it came to that. Martin would need to confirm both their whereabouts this morning. Leonard's as well. Cory, Russell Pedersson, and Richard Barnwell were others he'd need to chat with, given he suspected they were involved in Gary's little scheme to siphon gas from the UFA. The proof of that, Martin suspected, was still sitting in the tank on the back of Richard's truck.

Was he missing anyone else? Tyler. If he had killed Kristi in a jealous rage, would he do the same to the man he thought had driven them apart? He would if he still hadn't sobered up, Martin reasoned, which was a distinct possibility. Another name to be added to the pile.

Finally there was the question of Gary's nakedness to be added to the mountain of questions he had. What exactly did that imply? Had his killer surprised him somehow? Not without getting a key from Marshall, which he would have mentioned. Gary had let whomever it was in, then. Perhaps he had just gotten out of the shower when his killer arrived and knocked on the door. Wouldn't he put something on first? Maybe not if he knew who was there, though Martin found that hard to believe.

A woman and sex seemed the most likely explanation, given what he knew about Gary. Neither Karen nor Carol struck him as the sort of woman to find Gary attractive, but then, what did he know of such things? He considered and then dismissed the idea that someone had undressed Gary to cast suspicion in that direction. There was no blood on any of his clothes, and the scene in the bathroom did not suggest someone who had been moved.

Karen or Carol, then, assuming Tammy and Roxanne or some other woman scorned had not been involved. Karen had little motive that Martin could see. She had little motive to kill Kristi as well, given she had been the one to end the legal dispute with Kevin, and none to kill Gary that he knew. Carol had motive for both, and Martin did not trust her alibi for Kristi's death.

It occurred to him that he had only Karen's word that she had ended her involvement in the Mzikevitch family dispute. He knew who to check with to confirm that, and pulled out his phone to look for their numbers. As he did, he shook his head in disgust. "Goddamn idiot."

He had almost missed the obvious. Lara would not have missed something simple, and nor would any amateur detective watching procedurals on television, for that matter. He got out of the car and let himself back into the motel room, ripping the tape as he did so. Gary's phone sat on the table where Martin had left it after a cursory glance, the thought somehow not occurring to him to check and see who had called.

He flipped the phone open and fumbled a bit with the navigation before he got the trick of it. His own call had been the last Gary had received. In all likelihood he had been dead by then. There was one call thirty minutes before, a number that Martin recognized and which surprised him.

Leonard Taid. It could easily have been a business inquiry, Martin told himself. But it was certainly suspicious that one of his suspects in Kristi's murder had called Gary so near his own death. As he was still pursuing that line of thought, Gary's phone started to vibrate, and the God-awful squawking ringtone began to sound.

Without thinking, Martin set the phone down on the table, as though his mere touching of the device might alert whoever was calling to Gary's death. When it was through ringing, he picked it up and looked at the phone number, but did not immediately recognize it. Thirty seconds later it buzzed again, notifying him that a voicemail had been left.

It took him three tries to guess Gary's voicemail password. When he did, he heard the unmistakable deep intonations of Richard Barnwell. "Gary. Rich. Where you at? I know you said you'd call, but I can't be sitting here with that in my truck. How are we supposed to get rid of it?"

Martin did not hesitate, glancing first at the alarm clock on the bed to confirm the time. He texted Richard back in painstaking fashion, not bothering to fix his spelling errors: *Camt talk meet@1130@hotel.* Richard's reply was one letter: *K.*

Martin smiled to himself and went through the rest of Gary's logs. There were no outgoing calls and no text messages this morning. That left Roxanne, Marshall, and the caller as the only ones who definitely knew where Gary was this morning. He put Gary's phone in his pocket, went back outside, pulled the tape off the doors, and drove around front to talk to Marshall. He was sitting at the front desk, fidgeting and staring blankly at his crossword.

"You phone the custodian yet?" Martin said, taking the manager by surprise.

"Ye-eah, yeah," Marshall said, jumping up.

"You let anyone else know?"

Marshall solemnly shook his head.

"Good. Don't, at least not until I tell you you can. I have to let Roxanne know what's going on. If I find out that you or the custodian let slip what's happening here, I'll have you both arrested for interfering with an ongoing investigation."

Marshall's eyes widened at the threat, and he nodded vigorously. "Of course. Of course. I'll let Lina know right away too. No one will here from us."

"Good," Martin said with a nod of his own. "And if

anyone comes by looking for Gary, you just tell them that he left this morning. And then you call me and let me know who stopped by."

Martin did not wait for a response, turning and striding out into the snow, which continued to swirl. A single truck drove by, going slowly, as he made his way to his car, but other than that the streets were empty and silence reigned. He was almost to his car when his phone rang and he fumbled for it in his jacket, pulling it out to answer as he settled into his car seat and shut the door.

"Hello. Constable Martin here," he said.

"Hello," a voice with a German accent said. "This is Constable Martin, yes."

"Yes, Sam. How are you?"

"Fine, fine. I did some talking with the boys. They all swear up and down they haven't been out to the Johnstone coulee this winter. No traps."

Martin frowned, starting the car and flipping the wipers on to get rid of the accumulating snow. "And you believe them."

"Yeah, yeah. Someone would tell me if it wasn't true, you know. Someone would."

Martin thanked him and hung up, pursing his lips. If Sam was to be believed then someone else had been in the coulee that morning while he was talking to Leonard and Clarissa. Who could it have been? And why? The only conclusion he could come to was that there had to have been more than Kristi's body dumped in the coulee.

20

He had started down the street to the Hotel to confront Richard before he remembered that he had forgotten to phone the lawyers to see if they could confirm Karen's statements about withdrawing from the dispute with Kevin. August Jones was the only lawyer in town, but Victor Kerr worked out of Hanna and had a large client base here as well. He guessed Kristi and Karen would have been working with one, with Kevin retaining the other. Martin had August's number saved in his phone, so he pulled over to the side of the street and tried him first.

"August? Constable Martin here."

"What can I do for you today, constable?"

"I'm sure you've heard about Kristi Taid's death by now," Martin said, and heard a murmur of agreement on the other end. "I'm just following up on a number of leads at the moment. I wonder if you can tell me, had she and Karen retained you with regards to the case they were bringing against Kevin?"

There was a long pause on the other end as August weighed his words. "Obviously, I'm unable to discuss the details of our consultations on the matter. I can tell you that Karen and Kristi had approached me about contesting their father's will and Kevin's role as executor. If you want more detail than that, I'm afraid you'll have to talk with Karen directly."

"I understand completely, August, and I'll do that."

"Now, I should tell you that Kristi had indicated she was withdrawing from the case the day she died."

It was Martin's turn to fall silent. "Kristi had?" he managed at last.

"Yes, she phoned me that morning. She said she'd decided not to go forward with it."

"And Karen?"

"I haven't heard from her," August said. "As far as I know, the case is still going forward."

Martin thanked the lawyer for his time and hung up. He didn't move for some time, trying to process what he had just discovered. At last he reached out and shifted the car into park, letting it idle. He glanced at the clock to make sure he still had time to make it to the Hotel before Richard arrived. His chest felt constricted, and he started gasping for breath again and had to work to calm himself.

How many people had been lying to him and he had been oblivious?

"Don't be stupid," he told himself. "It was a damned foolish thing for her to do."

Why, then, had she? She would have to know that he would find out eventually, just like he had found out about the dispute in the first place. It only served to cast more suspicion on her motives and gained her, what—a few hours? Hardly enough to make a difference. The whole situation made little sense from her perspective, given that Karen had far less need of any settlement money they might get from Kevin than Kristi. Unless things were far less rosy than they appeared for the Mahls.

Martin shook his head and roused himself from the confused tangle of his thoughts. There would be time enough to deal with that. For now he had to get to the Hotel and meet with Richard. Hopefully the truck driver would be able to shed some light on Gary's business dealings in a way that wouldn't further complicate the investigation into his death.

Martin arrived at the Hotel just before 11:30 and found a booth in the near corner, where he had a view of the entrance and where whoever coming in wouldn't immediately spot him. He ordered a coffee from Lynn and then decided he might as well go ahead and order lunch as well. No sense in dealing with Richard and two murders on an empty stomach.

It was nearly quarter to twelve before Richard and Cory walked in, casting their eyes around the room. Richard froze when he noticed Martin, but Cory just smiled and waved. Effortlessly full of shit, Martin thought as he stood and waved them both over. They came, Cory all confidence, Richard trailing behind, his reluctance evident in his expression.

"You boys looking for someone?" Martin said, gesturing for them both to sit.

Cory slid into the booth without hesitation while Richard remained standing, looking as though he was contemplating running as far from this place as fast as he could. He was short, with broad shoulders and thick around the middle with a trucker's gut. His toque perched at an odd angle on the back of his head, looking as though it might slide off at any moment. He swept it off and ran a hand through the muss of his hair, still not meeting Martin's eyes.

"Go ahead," Martin said to him in a tone that indicated Richard had no choice in the matter. Only when the trucker sat down did Martin return to his own seat and look across at the two men, spinning his coffee cup in slow circles as he did so.

"So, gentlemen," Martin said. "Who are you here to meet?"

"We're supposed to be meeting with Gary," Cory said.

Richard gave a small nod of agreement. "Don't see him here, though."

"No," Martin said. "I haven't either. What were you meeting about?"

"He's just got some work for us," Cory said with a shrug. Richard gave him a look of warning. Lynn came by and they both ordered coffees, Cory enthusiastically adding sugar to his, Richard doing nothing with his, but fiddling with the spoon.

"What kind of work?" Martin said.

"Is that really any of your damn business?" Richard said. Cory gave a Martin a look, as though he didn't understand either why Richard was acting this way.

"What are you looking for Gary to help you get rid of?" Martin said. His question had the intended response, both men going very still.

"Gary tell you that?" Cory asked finally.

Martin shook his head.

"What the hell is going on?" Richard said, anger and panic warring in his voice.

"That's what I'd like to know, really," Martin said. "Why don't we start with what's in your truck? I think I know, but I'd like to hear it from you.

"And then we can get to what you're doing here with him?" he added, looking in Cory's direction, and had the satisfaction of seeing Cory go red in the face.

Richard cleared his throat. "Look, it was nothing, really. I just got some seed that I picked up and I was looking to swing a little deal."

"Spare me the bullshit. I know what was on the truck."

"Gary told you?" Cory said in disbelief.

"Gary's dead."

"No shit," Cory said, shaking his head. "What happened?"

Richard had gone very pale. Martin was worried he was going to faint in the chair.

"It looks like a homicide," Martin said, looking from

face to face. Both men appeared to be in a state of shock.

"Jesus Christ," Richard said. "I just saw him yesterday."

"You see him every day," Cory said.

"Not today," Richard said.

"You don't think we're suspects, do you?" Cory said, turning to Martin.

Martin shook his head. "No, but it's time to get down to brass tacks here. I need to know everything about your little scam with the gas. It may have a bearing on the case. So tell me everything, spare no details, and if I find out you've held back on me, I'll charge you both with obstruction of justice."

"It's nothing, really. I don't know what you've been told," Cory said. Richard shot him a look and he fell silent.

"We were the ones stealing gas from the UFA," Richard said, turning back to Martin. "It was Gary's idea. He told us when, he told us how. Everything."

"Fuck, man," Cory said, hitting Richard on shoulder. "What are you doing? We gotta get immunity and shit."

"Go on," Martin said, ignoring Cory's outburst.

Richard nodded, not even glancing in Cory's direction. "Right, so, Gary would tell me or Russell when to take it, usually at night, right around closing. Not so late that there would be questions if someone saw us. Then he'd tell us where to deliver it. Cash deal, right. We both got a cut."

"Who'd you sell the gas to?"

"Folks around here," Richard said. "Gary arranged all that too, right."

"What was your part in all this?" Martin said, looking at Cory. He refused to answer, staring off at the wall, a stormy expression on his face.

"He helped us," Richard said. "With the driving, with the deliveries. If one of us couldn't make it because we had to do a legitimate load, Cory would."

Martin nodded. "So the other night, then. You were at the bar with the boys and then left to go take the gas. Did you do that after Gary stopped by?"

"Yeah. He came by around eight or so, I guess to let me know it was on for ten. But he was a bit late coming back."

Lynn brought Martin's plate and he set it aside, his attention focused entirely on Richard. "Gary was there that night?"

"He was always there. He insisted. He was a little late, though. It was probably ten thirty by the time he got there."

"He give you a reason why?" Martin said. Richard shook his head and Martin sighed.

Cory sniffed at Martin's food. "You gonna eat that, man? It smells good."

"Just shut the fuck up and sit there if you're not going to be any help," Martin said, causing both men's eyes to widen. "Now, what did you both do when you were finished up?"

"Went our separate ways. Gary said he'd let me know tomorrow who the deliveries were for. But with the snow, he never did. That's why I called him this morning."

Martin took another sip of coffee, frowning. "What time did you finish up?"

"Eleven," Richard said with a shrug.

"I'm going to need the names. Who did you usually deliver to?"

Richard shook his head, sitting straight up.

Martin sighed. "How about this? I'll give you some names, and you nod if they got some gas."

Richard gave him a barely perceptible nod.

"Okay. Good. Leonard Taid. Wayne Johnstone. Kevin Mzikevitch. Arnold Mahl. Lyle Hargreaves."

The first and the last were the only nods he received from Richard. Martin was not surprised. It confirmed his thinking on the matter, at least to this point. If there were someone who was involved in both murders, as he still suspected was likely the case, then it would be one of those two. Either of them could have been present at the

Tea House when Kristi was killed. It remained to be seen if the same could be said of Gary, though Leonard's phone call was suggestive of something. Or perhaps nothing at all.

Cory and Richard were looking at each other as Martin pondered this and plotted his next steps, their discomfort plain on their faces. Martin had to resist a smile.

"Tell me, boys, do you think there was anything going on between Kristi and Gary?"

"Ty sure did," Cory said.

"Gary never said nothing. He was into that..." Richard hesitated.

"Tammy," Martin said flatly.

"Yeah, yeah. They had a thing. He and Kristi had some business, but honestly, I don't think it was anything like that. I know Ty did, but the truth is I think she was just tired of him, you know. A woman like that could do a lot better than Ty if she wanted to. I mean, she already had."

That she had, Martin thought. "So this thing with Kristi, you think was just business?"

Richard nodded. "Yeah, definitely. Gary's got his fingers in everyone's pies, you know. He's a devious kind, right. Was, I guess."

Martin nodded. So it seemed. He thanked them both and sent them on their way, saying they would discuss the theft of the gas later and that they should make sure they were available for the next few days. Both promised they would be, and they shuffled out of the Hotel heads low and looking embarrassed.

21

Martin finished his lunch, still mulling his next steps, deciding that he needed to first of all see if he could determine what he might have missed in the coulee. What was so important that the killer would risk returning to where the body had been dropped the next day? It could only be one thing, Martin realized. There had to be proof there of who had committed the crime that needed to be removed.

Martin decided he needed to go there first to determine if anything of use still remained. He had an idea of what it was, at least in part, and confirmation of that would be useful for the forensics team when they finally arrived. And if the killer had failed to remove everything, or had missed something. Confronting Karen with her further lies could wait. This might decide the case right here.

It was still snowing when he returned to his car, but the wind had died and the highway was relatively clear after the plowing that morning. As he drove, he checked back in with dispatch to see what the latest was on the forensics team and his backup support. Highway 9 had reopened, he was told, and an officer from Hanna was en route now, with the forensics team now expected that evening.

Constable Malback was the man being dispatched, he was told. Martin checked in with him directly and found out he had just left Hanna, which would put him two hours out, given the weather and the roads. Malback was new to the post and to the force, and Martin had never met him, but the prospect of anyone arriving to help in the investigation lifted his spirits immensely.

As he grew nearer to his destination, he pulled out his cell phone and dialed the Taids. Clarissa answered on the third ring.

"Do you want to talk with Dad?" she said after he had introduced himself.

"I do," he said. "Is he around?"

"No," she said. "You can try his cell, though. He had to go into town for some parts."

"What time did he go in?"

"Around nine, I guess. I don't think he's back yet."

He thanked her and said he would try him on his cell. Had he phoned Gary looking for parts, or was that simply to provide cover for his real intentions? And had those included murder?

It was possible Leonard had killed his wife, though Martin was still not clear on what his motive might be. Had he simply snapped after years of being played the fool? He did not strike Martin as that kind of person. So it was something else, something that Martin had failed, as yet, to turn up. He was in town while Gary was being murdered, knew about the stolen gas scheme, and potentially knew where Gary was staying, depending on the nature of their phone conversation. That was always tricky to assume, though.

The only thing Martin could say for certain was that Leonard could not have been the one to make the footprints he had seen. Those had been made when he was in Leonard's house talking with he and Clarissa. Even if Leonard had somehow managed to sneak out of the house without Martin becoming aware, he would not have had time to make his way over to the coulee and back.

The footsteps had come from the south anyway, and there had been no set of tracks returning. Whoever had made those tracks had still been there when Martin studied them, possibly watching him, hidden somewhere in the trees below. The thought left him chilled.

He passed the Johnstones' and came to the coulee, stopping along the side of the road. Wayne was at work in the corral adjacent, putting out bedding for the cattle, and he waved at Martin as he drove by in a tractor. Martin waved back and set out some traffic cones behind his car to go along with the hazards, in case there were others out on the road today. The snow persisted, and along with the low grey sky, it made it difficult to see into the distance.

When that was done, he made sure he had his radio with him and notified dispatch of what he was doing, asking them to check back in one hour. After some consideration, he decided to put a flak jacket on under his parka as well. Odds were there was no one waiting for him, no matter what evidence might remain down there. But on the off chance there was, better to be safe than sorry.

With the vest on under his parka and the radio turned up at his hip, he locked the car and plunged into the ditch, the snow rising to his thighs, and waded through it toward where he remembered Kristi's body being. The footprints had long ago vanished beneath the snow, as had the traffic cones he had left to mark where the body had been. The snow had drifted into banks and the entire landscape had changed, leaving him slightly disoriented.

What he was looking for did not lie there, though; it was below, where the footprints had gone. He made his way cautiously down the slope, grasping hold of the narrow trees that thrust their way up out of the coulee. As he went he looked for signs of what he suspected was there, but found nothing. It had all been covered by the snow, exactly as someone had hoped.

When he came to a point where the slope became too steep for him to continue, he stopped to assess the situation. He stared down the narrow crevice into the shadows and darkness where the trees, which seemed to lunge up out of the coulee, striving to escape its confines. Nothing revealed itself to his gaze, and he turned away, looking along the slope where the trees came almost to fence for Wayne's corral.

Whoever had passed through here that morning must have gone along the slope somewhere there. They could not have gone any farther than he had. Was there a pathway down? He decided to find out.

As he moved along the upper slope running nearly parallel with Wayne's fence, the pathway down became obvious. There were the outlines of a trail, hidden beneath all the snow, where the trees parted to allow passage in a series of switchbacks that gradually made their way down the slope. Perhaps the cattle had used this at one point; now it was left to the deer to wander. And whoever had made their way down here the day Kristi's body had been discovered.

His progress below was painstaking. With the trail obscured by snow, he took several paths that led to a sheltering of trees or a dead end and a precipitous drop. He slipped off the trail several times, skidding down the face of the coulee, trying desperately to stop himself and ending up covered from head to toe in snow. Then he had to climb back up to the path in order to continue on.

One of his falls led to him losing his cell phone. It had been in one of his jacket pockets, which he thought he had zipped up, but evidently had not. He conducted a frantic search of his immediate surroundings, made more difficult by the fact that he could barely stay balanced on the slope where he was. After a few minutes he abandoned his attempt, deciding he was more likely to slide further down the slope and away from the path than he was to actually find the phone in the snow. The radio would suffice for contact with the outside world while he was down here.

By the time he reached the bottom, he was exhausted and shivering from his damp clothes and the cold. The coulee was wider than he had expected, the cliffs on either side bowing out, especially with their blanket of trees, to obscure most of what lay below. That included the thin creek that snaked its way through the ravine. The ice on it had yet to entirely break away, but he could hear the lulling rush of its water as it passed by. It was so narrow that it seemed impossible to believe its passage had carved this valley from the earth. The quiet and stillness was deep here, far below the highway and away from both the Johnstone and Taid yards, and the snow muffling everything as well. He stood for a moment and took it in, letting the hush settle over him.

In coming down he had gone about half a mile north of the highway, and now had to trek back through snow that was waist deep in some places. He tried to stay as near to the creek as possible, but it was still hard going. More than an hour had passed since he started his descent, and the lengthening shadows around him, along with the continuing snow, made him somewhat concerned about his return journey to the ridge above.

His concern only grew as he realized that he had heard no reports from the radio as to Malback's progress or that of the forensics team. Dispatch should have checked in with him by now to ensure everything was fine. He fiddled with the radio for a bit, trying to send and checking for reception, to no avail. Water from the snow must have got in somewhere, or the signal was being cut off from somewhere down here. Either way, he was now utterly alone.

He nearly missed what he had come looking for, as he approached where the coulee turned to run parallel with the highway above, the snowdrifts so high that it was a struggle to just move forward, let alone observe what was around him. Partly it was that he had expected it to be further ahead, nearer to where he judged the highway above to be. It was only the oddness of its shape, so incongruous amidst this idyllic valley, near a creek and surrounded by trees, that made him stop to look again. When he did, he wondered how he could have missed it in the first place.

It was blanketed in snow and crumpled oddly, but still unmistakably a car. Kristi Taid's car. He felt a surge of exultation at having been correct in his assumption. It was clear now what had happened. The body had not been dumped, the car with the body in it had. Somehow, as the car rolled into the coulee, the body had fallen from the vehicle. Martin guessed that whoever had pushed the car in had not closed the door properly after locking the steering wheel, and had not bothered with a seatbelt for the body. And the darkness had not allowed them to realize their mistake.

That was important as well, for there could be no doubt now that more than one person was involved in Kristi's death. There had to be two. The person who had driven Kristi's car with the body out to be dumped in the coulee, and the one who had picked the driver up. As he brushed the snow away from the door, he tried to think of who among his suspects could have worked together.

Lyle and Carol seemed obvious, the rest less so. Had Gary been one of them, and had his murder been a consequence of his involvement?

It was unlikely Martin would find answers here, though perhaps the forensics team could. He wondered if there was a simpler way for them to get here than the trail he had taken. The coulee, after all, must lead somewhere. He could ask Wayne when he returned above.

He put that thought aside for the moment and brushed the snow from the car so that he could get one of the doors open. Miraculously, none of the windows had broken in the car's long fall down the cliff, though he could see the windshield was badly cracked when he managed to get the passenger door open. As a result, there was no snow in the car to contaminate the scene.

In fact, there was nothing at all in the car. Martin had not seen a cleaner vehicle, except perhaps Gary's this morning. There was none of the usual detritus that people naturally accumulated: no change or pens, no receipts, not even a travel mug. The light was poor, but he thought he could see stains on the passenger seat. He could not be certain they were blood, though he suspected they were.

What seemed beyond question was that the car had been cleaned, most likely before it had been pushed down the coulee. Which led to the question of why anyone would return to the coulee the next day, given it would potentially leave a trail of evidence to them. Something had been missed, something that could not be left behind.

He was pondering various possibilities of what that could be when the gunshot sounded, echoing through the coulee. The hiss of the bullet, near enough that he could almost feel its passage through the air, caused his heart to wrench. He whirled around to face his attacker, but all he saw was the empty coulee bottom looking as idyllic as before, with the trees and the creek and the snow slowly descending.

Somewhere in the trees, was his thought, as the second and third shots rang out in quick succession. Both struck him, one in the chest near his heart, the impact absorbed by the vest, the other in the right shoulder just below where the vest stopped. He lay on the ground stunned for a moment, waves of pain ricocheting through him, trying to assemble a coherent response to what was happening.

The shots came from very close by, just off to his right. He needed to return fire, he realized, and struggled to raise himself up so he could get to his gun. Agony coursed through him as he put the full weight of his body on his injured arm and collapsed back to the ground, groaning miserably. He briefly wondered, given the pain in his chest that came with each breath, if the vest had stopped the bullet there. Just a broken rib, he told himself, as he tried to pull his gun free with his injured arm.

There were no further shots, but he was certain he could hear the distinctive crunch of footsteps through the snow over his ragged and desperate breathing. He managed to clasp his gun in his hand, keeping it low to his side in case whoever had shot him was approaching. The sound of the footsteps grew louder and louder, his assailant growing nearer and nearer. He thought about raising his head to catch a glimpse of whoever it was, but decided it was better to wait until the last possible moment.

His attacker denied him that chance, changing paths and looping around the car so that he could come up on Martin from behind. Knowing he had little time, Martin tried frantically to lever himself up so that he could face his assailant and get a shot off. The pain was extraordinary, and he was unable to stop himself from crying out as he pushed himself up into a half-sitting position. His vision went black, and he thought for a moment he might vomit.

Through the dimness of his pain, Martin could hear his attacker hurrying around the car toward him. Knowing he had little time, he raised his arm up as best he could and fired off two shots wildly. The air sang as the bullets pierced its nothingness and landed far away, leaving only echoes in their wake. It was all he could manage before the pain forced him to drop his arm back to his side.

His assailant was upon him before he had time to gather himself again. Martin could only manage a glimpse at jeans tucked into thick-soled green work boots, when the butt of the rifle landed square in his eye, sending colors spinning wildly until blackness mercifully descended.

22

Martin emerged from darkness to the sound of another shot echoing through the valley, some distance from where he lay upon the snow. It took a moment for it to register in his mind and to comprehend what it meant. There was someone else in valley, and whoever it was might have just been shot by his assailant. He tried to sit, and blacked out again.

He came to moments later, his head feeling as though it had been cleaved in two, and one half of it lay on the other side of the car. For some reason, the fact that he had forgotten to phone Roxanne Seedstrom and notify her of her husband's murder surfaced in his mind. Word might have spread to her by now. She was a suspect as well, maybe the obvious one. But nothing was obvious here.

Martin shook his head, to clear the fog from his mind, to little effect. Roxanne wasn't Gary's killer. Whoever had killed Gary had just shot him. It was all tied up in this Kristi mess, the stain of which seemed to be spreading further and further, like his blood upon the snow.

Moving with care now, trying not to give in to the urgency he felt, he pulled himself up into a sitting position, propping his back against the car. Both doors on his side of the car had been left open, so whoever had attacked him had taken the time to conduct a search before leaving. Martin wondered if his assailant had come away as empty-handed as he had.

When the world seemed a little more stable, the snow no longer moving in circles before his eyes, he used the car to get to his feet. He glanced at his shoulder and saw that his jacket was red and damp with blood. Taking his glove off, he put a finger to the wound. There was enough blood to be worrisome, but not enough for an artery to be involved. He tried to grip his gun and raise it to a firing position and nearly passed out from the pain, slumping against the car to support himself. He closed his eyes, gathered himself, and tried again, this time managing it, though just barely, his hand shaking badly. It would have to do.

He set off back along the trail he had already broken, moving at an agonizingly slow pace. Each breath hurt, and his head and arm were throbbing. Glancing behind him, he could see the trail of blood he was leaving behind, and he was filled with a sudden certainty that he was being stalked by a coyote, even as he stalked his assailant. He whirled around to confront the beast, raising his gun to fire at it, crying out in pain as he did so. All that he could see were the trees, the creek, and the car, the only sound the silence of the falling snow.

Shaking his head, he pressed on, trying to ignore the pain and the flashes of color that crept into the corners of his vision. He kept his eyes focused on the trail ahead and thought he could make out where his assailant had trekked in, following Martin's path right up to the car, evidently. How had he not heard him? His own footsteps must have obscured the others.

He was not certain how he was going to manage any confrontation he found himself in, given his current state. But it was unlikely to be an issue, given the pace he was able to maintain. More important now was how he was going to get out of the coulee. He wasn't sure he could manage a climb back up the slope, so he would have to try walking out of the coulee bottom, a dangerous proposition, given he had no idea how far it went or where he would be when he emerged from it.

Malbeck should have arrived by now, and hopefully would have gone out to investigate after Martin missed his callback with the dispatch. When he found the car, would he be able to determine where Martin had gone?

His trail should still be visible, even with the snow, and he could enlist Wayne Johnstone to direct him, as Martin should have. Perhaps he already had, and maybe that was why there had been another shot. The thought made him shiver.

When he came to where he had descended from the slope, another trail continued on, following the creek's path, and he kept on it. Whoever his assailant was—presumably the same person who had left the trail down the slope he had seen that morning—had to know the coulee well. Leonard Taid fit that bill, of course, having spent his entire life beside the coulee, but it was impossible for him to have made those footprints. Who else knew this area that well?

The creek, and the coulee with it, curved up ahead, nearly doubling back on itself. As Martin followed the path that had been broken around the bend he came upon Wayne Johnstone, slumped limply into a snowdrift, his mouth hanging open. Martin ran toward him, plunging through the snow, ignoring the agony in his chest.

"What happened?" he said as he came up to stand over him. Wayne opened his eyes slightly, appearing not to recognize him. There was blood on the snow around him, running down the center of his jacket.

"Jesus," Martin said.

"Hell of a thing," Wayne murmured. "Hell of a thing."

Martin slipped his gun back in his holster and crouched over Wayne, trying to assess his wound. The light and his layers of clothes made it difficult. He swore under his breath and tried the radio again, but he could not even hear static in response.

"Talk to me, Wayne," he said as he took off his gloves and began to rummage through the rancher's pockets. "Stay with me."

"Can't believe he shot me."

"Who shot you?" Martin said, giving a grunt of triumph as he found Wayne's cell phone attached to his belt.

"Why would he do that?" Wayne's voice was very faint. He sounded confused.

"Who did it?" Martin said, only half paying attention as he dialed the number for dispatch.

"Hell of thing. After everything, you know, I done for him."

Each ring of the phone was agony as Martin waited for someone to pick up. Wayne kept repeating what he had already said, more or less, as Martin got through, notified dispatch of what had happened, and asked them to relay it to Malbeck.

"Don't bother with sending an ambulance. It won't get here in time. I'm going to get to Wayne's truck and go from there."

He paused and looked down at Wayne, who repeated, "After everything I done for him."

When Martin was done with the dispatcher, he dialed again. "Diane? Martin. Wayne's been shot, Diane," he said without preamble. "We're down in the coulee. I'm going to try to bring him to his truck, but I don't know how far that is. Meet us there if you can. Okay. And if you see anyone on the roads, whoever it is, stay clear."

Martin slipped the phone into his pocket and took care to do the zipper up. He looked up at the sky, grimacing at the still-descending snow and the growing darkness. It would be nightfall by the time he managed to get Wayne out of the coulee. He crouched over him and looked at the wound again, debating about asking if he could feel his legs. In the end, Martin decided against it. It didn't matter anyway. They didn't have time to wait for an ambulance; Wayne had to be moved now if was going to survive.

Though it was pure agony, so much so that he nearly blacked out in his initial attempt, Martin managed to lift Wayne up under his good shoulder. After collecting himself for a moment and waiting for the flashes of color and darkness to go from his eyesight, Martin set off on the trail Wayne and their assailant had broken. He stumbled with every step, Wayne's weight and his own injuries throwing him off balance. More than once he fell, sending them both toppling into the snow, and had to grit his teeth and drag himself and the rancher back up again.

Their progress was achingly slow, and with every minute that passed, Martin felt his own strength draining, like the light that was leaving the sky, both of them marking the dwindling time Wayne had left to him. In spite of his wound and their falls, Wayne kept up his aimless chatter, his voice not faltering. Martin took that as a sign that there was still time left, and redoubled his efforts.

But each step now seemed more difficult, and it was getting harder and harder to maintain his focus. He needed to be going forward, step by step, following the trail, to get out of the coulee and find Diane. But his mind kept flitting away from his present moment. He thought of Gary, naked and bloody upon the toilet, and Roxanne, brittle with barely contained anger. Had she broken after he left her and gone to find Gary?

The longer he thought about it, the more certain he was. She had motive and she had opportunity. It had been a mistake not to talk to her immediately. Instead, he had gone running off into this coulee and gotten himself shot. And Wayne too.

Lara would not have made such a foolish mistake. She would have known to follow procedure, that with the storm time was on their side. Whoever had killed Kristi wasn't going anywhere. Nor was her vehicle. He had let it all go wrong.

After what seemed like hours struggling through the snow, his breath becoming ragged and his sight dimming to the point where he could only see what was immediately in front of him, he heard a cry. It so startled him that he nearly dropped Wayne and tried to reach for his gun before his senses recovered. He looked up to see Diane running toward them, her face ashen.

"My God, my God," she said, as she came to them, out of breath herself. "What a sight you are."

Martin tried to reply, but the words would not come, his brain stagnant, his whole body numb.

"Stay with me, both of you," Diane said, slipping herself under Wayne's other arm to support him. "It's not far now," she said, looking over at Martin, who nodded dumbly at her.

Diane nodded in turn, and with that they set off into the growing darkness and the steadily falling snow.

23

Martin did not remember reaching the truck, nor could he recall much of their frantic journey into town, Diane driving far too quickly, given the condition of the roads. The truck skidded and slipped, nearly drifting off the highway at times, though Diane always managed to bring it under control. She brought them to the hospital, where Botha was waiting and rushed Wayne in to try to stabilize him.

Normally the STARS air ambulance helicopter would have been summoned for a patient as critical as Wayne was, but with the storm that was impossible. Once he was stabilized as best Botha could manage, Cory and Diane headed off in the ambulance with Wayne and one of the nurses for Medicine Hat, where they would perform surgery—if Wayne managed to last that long. It seemed grim.

Botha tended to Martin's injuries, which were nowhere near as serious. As he had suspected, the bullet wound in his arm had caught mostly muscle and passed completely through, so it was a simple thing to deal with. And his broken or bruised ribs were taped up, there being little more that could be done with them. He had a concussion as well, Botha informed him, so he was not to attempt anything too strenuous in the next few days.

Malbeck found him as he was recovering in bed. "Quite the near thing," he said, nodding at Martin. "Good thing you were wearing the vest."

"Just lucky I was," Martin said, shaking his head. "I had no reason to know someone would be down there."

"I take it you didn't get a look at who it was?"

Martin shook his head. "Just some boots. Green winter work boots. They sell them at the UFA. Anybody could have a pair. Wayne saw him. He knows."

"We'll be lucky if he survives to make an identification," Malbeck said. "In the meantime, we've got a killer on the loose."

"Maybe more than one," Martin said, frowning.

"Any ideas as to a suspect?"

"Too goddamn many," Martin said. "Too goddamn many."

He reflected for a moment on what Wayne had said when he discovered him. *After all I done for him.* Leonard was the obvious candidate, given they were neighbors and would have helped each other plenty over the years. And his whereabouts were unaccounted for, unless there was someone in town who had seen him after two or three.

"Leonard Taid has to be the main suspect here," he said, and explained why to Malbeck. "But I don't think he killed his wife. I mean, I've got nothing to exclude him specifically, but it's just a feeling. There's no reason I can see for him to do it. And he couldn't have been the one who left the tracks into the coulee that first day."

Malbeck shot him a questioning look, and Martin explained that as well. How someone had gone down into the coulee the morning the body was discovered, just after Cory had taken it away, in point of fact, and how that had led him to realize there had to be some kind of evidence down there—Kristi's car, most likely. Whoever had gone down there that first morning had returned today. But to what purpose?

"By the way, the forensics team got in tonight," Malbeck said. "They've started on the hotel room where you found Gary Seedstrom. They'll finish that tonight and start on the car and that whole mess tomorrow once it's light."

Martin nodded, only half listening to what Malbeck said. Why had someone returned to the car a second time? What could have been there that they had left behind, that they hadn't gotten the first time, or that first night when the body was dumped? He tried to recall what the vehicle had looked like when he studied it, fighting through the fog of his memory. The afternoon seemed a lifetime ago now, but he could recall the car. It had been clean, empty of anything.

"Fuck me," he said, shaking his head.

"You all right?" Malbeck said.

Martin nodded grimly, holding up a hand to forestall any more questions. He needed to think. There had been two people who had gone into the coulee. The first had found a way down from the highway, as Martin had. That person had been unfamiliar with the coulee, otherwise they would have known about the entrance at the bottom. So two people, both looking for the same thing. Kristi's purse, or something in the car that had been missed. Something that could link them to the crime.

The car had been clean when he found it, nothing to implicate anyone that he had seen, though he had not checked the trunk. But it seemed to him there was unlikely to be anything there, which meant the first person to make the trek below had retrieved whatever was there. The second trip by someone else suggested that those involved in killing Kristi Taid were not working in concert, or at least not sharing all they knew.

He racked his brain, trying to think of what might have been missed on their first cleaning of the car. His head ached with the effort, and he closed his eyes, feeling his nausea rise again. Malbeck was watching him curiously, he saw when he opened his eyes, and Martin tried to explain his thinking to him.

Malbeck nodded along with his reasoning. "I agree," he said, pursing his lips. "Has to be two people who went down there. Who could it be? You say the first time couldn't be Leonard? What about your other guys?"

"Not Gary," Martin said. "He needed to be at the gas bar in the morning to call in the theft. Lyle, potentially."

"Okay, anyone else potentially?"

Martin shrugged. "Maybe. Karen, or Arnold maybe, but I can't see either of them being in good enough shape to make that trip down the coulee. It was a hell of a lot of work."

Malbeck nodded, pulling out his notebook. "Okay. So I get Lyle's alibi for the morning after Kristi Taid's death. And I guess his alibi for today too. Now who else could have come by this afternoon? Leonard. This Karen and Arnold? And are any of these connected to Gary?"

Martin winced, his thoughts seizing up and refusing to form into anything useful. He could feel his pulse on the side of his head, a steady, repetitive ache that refused to subside. Exhaustion from his afternoon's exertions settled upon him and he lay back on the bed.

Malbeck cleared his throat uncomfortably. "Look, I'll follow up with the forensics team and maybe check in on some of these alibis. You get some rest here."

Martin nodded, unable to summon the strength even for a reply. Malbeck ducked out of the room, leaving him alone. Martin listened as the constable's footsteps echoed down the corridor of the hospital, his eyes staring off at nothing, his mind absent of thought.

24

Martin did not know how long he lay there staring at the blank white hospital wall, unable to summon a thought. In spite of his exhaustion he was unable to find sleep, the throb of his various injuries not helping in that regard. He tried counting up and down, tried focusing on his breathing, all to no avail. In the end he simply stopped trying, and started to go over the case again in his own mind.

The two trips into the coulee continued to confound him, as did the question of what they could have been looking for, so he decided to put that aside and look at Gary's murder and any possible connections it might have to Kristi's. There seemed little doubt that Gary had been present during Kristi's final moments, though whether he had witnessed or participated in her murder was an open question.

There could be no question that their lives had intersected in several ways. Both Tyler and Tammy had believed there was an affair. And Tyler and Lyle had said the two were conspiring to raise the rent on the Tea House to force Carol out of the business. That aspect confused Martin somewhat, for he couldn't see Gary's end in things.

All he would gain in doing that was attention for himself and his relationship with Kristi, which, given Roxanne's reaction, was not something he would want at all.

There was also the fact that both Leonard and Lyle were buyers of his stolen gas. Had Kristi been aware of this little scheme? Or Carol? It would have been a difficult thing to keep from them, but Martin did not see how it might intersect with their other dealings.

As Martin thought everything through, an idea gradually began to shape itself in his mind. He sat up in bed, wincing in pain as he did so, but feeling a surge of adrenaline as well as certainty began to take hold. He needed to get in touch with Malbeck. His cell phone was lost to the coulee, he recalled, and he did not know the constable's number. He thought for a moment before arriving at a decision, rolling gingerly out of bed and walking out to the front desk.

The nurse on hand, whose name he struggled to remember, looked startled to see him. "Constable, you should be in bed."

"Where's my jacket?" he said. "It's not in the room."

"I guess they had to cut it off you. Do you want to call Dr. Botha? He's gone home for the night, but…"

Martin shook his head. "I need to get in touch with Constable Malbeck."

She looked blankly at him.

"I just need your phone, please."

She nodded and gestured for him to come around the desk. He called up dispatch and had them pass on a message to the constable to come by the hospital to pick him up, and to bring a jacket. Malbeck arrived fifteen minutes later, looking as concerned as the two nurses on duty, who kept conferring at the desk as he sat in one of the chairs in the waiting area, staring blankly at the wall.

"You should be in bed, Martin," Malbeck said. "Doctor's orders."

"I think I know what happened," he said. "Did you

bring a jacket?"

"I'm not taking you out of here. The doctor said you're not fit for duty."

"We need to go talk to Russell Pedersson. He knows what's going on."

"All right," Malbeck said, putting a guiding hand on Martin's shoulder. "You tell me what I need to ask him and I'll do it tonight. As soon as you get back into bed."

Martin shrugged off Malbeck's hand in irritation and headed out of the waiting area to the hospital doors, which slid open as he approached.

"Martin, come on," Malbeck said, moving to intercept him.

Martin would not be denied. "No, you come on. We'll stop by my place to get my other jacket. And then we can go get one of the forensics guys. I won't carry and I'll be an off-duty observer, or whatever you want to call it, if shooting starts."

Malbeck sighed in exasperation, biting at his lip. He looked as though he very much wanted to say no, but knew there was no stopping Martin, and so he nodded and the two of them walked out of the hospital into the cold of the night.

Martin shifted uncomfortably in his seat, his jacket not sitting right on his shoulders with his arm tied in a sling. He had been very careful getting in and out of the car to hide how much pain he was actually in from Malbeck, but he suspected the constable knew very well. From his place they had gone to the Deerfoot Inn, where the forensics team was still working. The lead on the team had reluctantly agreed to let go of one of his people, a young woman named Grenier, and she now sat in the back seat looking out the window as Martin directed Malbeck to Russell Pedersson's house.

It was on the outskirts of town, on the east side of the railway tracks, where the 891 curved to link up with the 41.

Though the elevators had been shuttered and torn down in the last few years, there was still the seed and fertilizer plants, as well as a scattering of houses and yards where people stored machinery. Russell's was a combination of both, with his house at the front of the property and an equipment shed at the back where he kept his backhoe, grain liner, and other assorted equipment that he either rented out or sold his services for.

"This guy likely to be armed?" Grenier said, her first words since entering the car, as Malbeck pulled into his driveway.

"He'll have a few guns," Martin said. "Everybody here does. But he knows I've got something else to talk him about. And he's not a suspect here."

"That you know of," Malbeck said as he turned the car off. He turned back to look at Grenier. "Let's not take any chances, shall we?"

Martin hid his irritation, masking it with the pain that enveloped him as he got out of the car. Malbeck was right, he knew, especially after what had happened these last two days. He might think he knew these people and what they were capable of, but events had proven him terribly wrong.

The three of them walked to the house, Malbeck going up the steps to the door, Grenier and Martin standing below to wait. Grenier put a hand on her gun as Malbeck knocked on the door. There was no response from within, though there were lights on throughout the house. Martin tried, but failed, to see anything through the front windows. Malbeck glanced down at him, and he shrugged in response.

Malbeck nodded and knocked again. "Russell Pedersson. This is Constable Malbeck. I have a few questions I'd like to ask you. Why don't you come out and talk?"

A screen door banged on other side of the house, and they could all hear a muffled curse. Malbeck was down the steps in a bound, drawing his gun and flashlight from his belt. Grenier had done the same, and he motioned for her to go down one side while he took the other.

"You stay here."

Martin nodded. He had no intention of following them, knowing he would only be a hindrance to any pursuit, and a worry to two officers who needed to be focused on the whoever was fleeing the scene. He pulled the radio from his belt so that he could be ready to report to them if Pedersson somehow managed to elude them and make his way back here.

With that done, he waited, cocking his head to listen. He could hear the dim crunch of two pairs of footsteps in the snow until even that disappeared into the night, leaving only the muffled quiet of the descending snow. Martin closed his eyes and could visualize what was happening: Malbeck and Grenier meeting at the other side of the house and following the tracks in the snow to the equipment shed. There was what he thought was the sound of a door being opened, he assumed to the equipment shed, followed by more silence.

After about ten minutes, his radio crackled to life. "Shed is clear. Tracks lead out into the field. What's out there?"

Martin struggled to recall what was on the other side of Russell's house, before replying, "It's just a field. A couple of them. Nothing out there for a couple of miles at least."

"We're going to pursue on foot. We'll report in every five minutes. Have dispatch contact the forensics team to inform them of the situation. Await further instruction."

Martin acknowledged Malbeck's report and radioed dispatch to have them contact the forensics team. A response came, just before Malbeck's own report, that some of the team would be coming by in support shortly. After informing Malbeck, Martin idled in front of the house, still listening for signs of somebody returning, but relaxed now, not expecting anything. As the tension left him, leaving only pain from his injuries, the chill of the night, and boredom, he decided it wouldn't hurt to head inside to see what was in there.

He went up the steps and tried the door, and was unsurprised to find it open. Stepping inside to the front porch, he kicked the snow off his boots and called out, "Hey, Russell."

There was no response, and he nodded to himself as he shut the door behind him. He decided against taking his boots off. The situation might require him to move quickly, and Russell deserved his floor getting dirtied, at least, for running when the cops showed up. He knew better than that.

From the porch to Martin's left there was a bathroom and what he assumed was a bedroom with its door shut. A short corridor, lined with a long closet, ran straight ahead, leading to the rest of the house. Martin took a couple of steps down the corridor and then stopped, cocking his head, certain he had heard something. He stood, holding his breath, waiting until it came again, a muffled cry, very faint, from behind the bedroom door.

Malbeck's report came in as Martin was debating whether he had in fact heard anything, and when he responded to it, the cry grew slightly louder, sounding strained and frantic. He went to the bedroom, throwing the door open and finding the light switch on the wall, revealing Tammy lying naked on the bed, her wrists and ankles bound together with a shirt, and what looked like her own panties gagging her mouth. Martin ran to her, removing the gag from her mouth, and started to work on the knots that bound her.

"Where's Russell?" he said, as Tammy sobbed in relief.

"I don't know," she managed to say, her breath coming in gasps. "He took him."

Martin succeeded in getting the shirt untied—one of Russell's work shirts, by the look of it—and handed it to her to put on. She struggled into it, her whole body shaking uncontrollably.

"Just breathe. Breathe. In and out," he said, as he looked her over for any injuries and was relieved to see none. "Who took him?"

"Lyle. He just busted in here. We were…and he had a gun…then he made Russ tie me up, and then he took him."

Martin looked around the room for her underwear and pants while he relayed to Malbeck over the radio that he was in pursuit of Lyle Hargreaves and that Russell Pedersson was currently missing.

"Acknowledged. Wait for backup before you enter the house," was Malbeck's response. Martin allowed himself a roll of the eyes at Tammy, who looked blankly at him, still terrified.

"It's all right," he said as he handed her the clothes. "Just breathe. Focus on that. We're going to find Russ. There's more police on their way. Okay?"

Tammy nodded and slipped into the rest of her clothes, doing up the buttons on Russ's shirt with fumbling hands.

"What time did you get here?" Martin said, as helped her to her feet from the bed.

"I came by right after work."

"After eight, then," Martin said. "And what time did Lyle come by?"

"I…I didn't really notice the time," Tammy said, going red.

"Okay. So he made Russell tie you up and then he took Russell. How long do you think you were tied up?"

She rubbed her wrists. "Half an hour," she said, sounding doubtful.

"What did Lyle say?" he said, leading her from the bedroom and down the corridor.

Tammy shook her head. "He was just yelling and…I don't, I don't really remember."

"That's okay," Martin said. "That's okay. Did you hear anything else when you were in there? Did you hear them leave the house? Or come back?"

She thought for a moment. "I heard you come in, but that was it."

Martin nodded, not looking at her, as he stepped from the hallway into the kitchen. Russell sat slumped in a chair by the table, his face bruised, a small pool of blood collecting on the linoleum around his feet. His hands were tied behind his back and he was naked. Behind him Martin heard Tammy make an odd, strangled sound. He turned to see her staring at Russell in horror, her hands at her mouth.

"Call Botha," he said. "Tell him to get here right away. You know his number?"

She shook her head, and Martin called it out to her as he walked over to check on Russell. His breathing was shallow but steady, and his pulse was strong. Martin looked for the source of the blood and saw that the ear on the far side of his head had been cut off. Glancing between his legs, Martin could see that there was a slash on one of his thighs, very near his testicles, where a steady drip of blood still flowed.

"Oh God, is he gonna die?" Tammy said, standing beside Martin and staring down at Russell's wounds.

"Call Botha," he said, and repeated the number. "Tell him he needs to get here as soon as possible. Okay?"

He guided her away from the body, pushing her to the phone hanging on the wall. She picked it up and started to dial. Martin went behind Russell's chair, crouching down to untie his hands, wincing in pain. When he got the knots loose, he took the shirt and bound it around Russell's thigh, as tight as he could manage given he only had one arm to use. It would have to do for now.

"He said he'll be here in fifteen minutes," Tammy said, hanging up.

"Good," Martin said, pondering his next step. It had been more than five minutes since Malbeck had called in, he realized, and he radioed out asking for a response.

There was none, and he tried again, swearing under his breath. After three tries he notified dispatch that they were non-responsive, and asked for the forensics team to respond immediately.

What now, he wondered, biting at his lip. If Lyle had somehow gotten the jump on Malbeck and Grenier, would he return here or keep running? He might come back. He wouldn't know about the forensics team, and he would probably assume that Martin was either dead or in the hospital. The house would presumably be empty, except for the prisoners he had left, and he could return for what he had come for.

25

Martin realized he did not have much time if Lyle was indeed returning to the house. The forensics team was also coming, as was Botha. But would they arrive before Hargreaves? It seemed unlikely.

He turned to Tammy, who was staring at him wide-eyed, the same realization settling upon her. "Go back into the bedroom now," he said. "Lock the door if it has one. Get behind the bed, or under it if you can. Wait there until I come and get you. Whatever you do, don't come out unless I or another police officer says to."

She gave a kind of half-swallow, half-gasp and fled from the kitchen, giving Russell a last terrified glance before she left. Martin could hear her shutting the door, and when he was certain she was safely out of the way, he pulled out a chair and sat opposite Russell. He tried again to raise Malbeck or Grenier on the radio, but all he received in reply was static. His mouth felt dry and he wanted to go to the sink for water, but he decided that would not be wise. He didn't want Lyle to see him as he approached.

As he glanced at the clock on the stove, which read 10:32, he heard the back door open and close with a thud, followed by footsteps down the hall. They came nearer, sounding wet with snow, and Lyle Hargreaves came around the corner and into the kitchen, coming to a sudden halt as he realized Martin was there. Hargreaves carried a rifle in one hand, the muzzle pointing at the ground. As he registered Martin's presence, he brought the gun up to his shoulder to take aim.

"Don't bother, Lyle," Martin said, trying to keep his voice even. "It's over."

"What's over?" Lyle said.

Martin noted the tension heavy in Lyle's voice. He was desperate, which meant Martin would have to be very careful.

"This whole goddamn mess, Lyle," Martin said, gesturing over to Russell. "What'd you do to those other two officers?"

"Jumped them. Knocked them cold with the rifle butt. They'll be fine when they come to. Wish I could say the same for you, Martin. It's too bad. I always liked you."

He spoke with a wistfulness that made Martin's blood go cold. "You damned near killed me once. Don't add another couple of bodies to your total. Not now. You can't get away with it."

"Why not? I kill you, I kill this piece of shit," Lyle said, pointing his gun at Russell, "and the slut in the bedroom, and who would even know I'm here?"

"The forensics team will. The same way they'll know you were in Gary's motel room, and out back where you shot Kristi. In her car, too. Maybe even where you dumped her body."

Lyle shook his head in disgust. "I had nothing to do with Kristi. That was Gary and Carol's doing. Their little scheme."

"So when Carol called you that night, it was to tell you they'd killed Kristi."

"She told me she had done it. What nonsense. She's never fired a gun in her life. And then Gary and I got rid of the body. But that asshole couldn't even manage that properly. Maybe he never intended to. He was trying to pin it all on me, and like a fool, I played right along."

Martin nodded, hoping to keep Lyle talking until the forensics team arrived. Where the hell were they? His hands were shaking, he realized, and pressed against his body to hide the fact.

He took a stab in the dark next. "So everybody was talking about Kristi and Gary, but it was Carol, wasn't it? She was trying to get Kristi out, and Gary was helping her to do it."

"He was doing a hell of a lot more than that," Lyle said, his voice trembling with emotion. "Look, I don't have time for this, Martin. I need to end this all tonight, find the documents this asshole wouldn't tell me about, and wrap things up."

There was something ominous about the way he said those last words that made Martin wonder if Carol was still alive. He didn't ask. Instead he lied. "They were in her jacket pocket. Not in the car, not in her purse."

Lyle looked defeated. "Christ, there's no getting Carol out of this, is there?"

"I'm afraid not," Martin said. "Why'd they kill her, if they were trying to squeeze her?"

Lyle shrugged, as though he would be the last person to know. "She wasn't going along with their little play, I guess. They gave her documents to sign to sell her half, and she wouldn't do it. Told Gary to raise the lease. You can't bluff her."

"So they decided to get rid of two problems at once," Martin said, nodding toward Lyle.

"Yeah, yeah," Lyle said, tears in his voice. "They used my gun. Had me help them dispose of the body, because I'm a goddamn idiot."

Martin had to remind himself to breathe. It felt like he was watching someone disintegrate before his very eyes. He kept listening for the sound of cars approaching, or for the flash of lights in the window, knowing that he would have to be ready to move when it came. Lyle was blocking the one exit, but there was another behind him leading into the living room, which Martin hoped would connect out to the hallway and the back door. It was his only option.

Where the hell was the forensics team? It felt like fifteen minutes had passed.

"So you killed Gary, then?"

Lyle gave a jerky nod. "Yeah. Had to. Couldn't trust him to not try to sell us out to save his own skin."

And because of Carol, Martin thought, but did not say. He could not resist a glance at the clock, and saw it click over to 10:41. Lyle followed his gaze and tightened his grip on the rifle, raising the sight up to his eyes.

"Who the hell you waiting for, Martin?"

As he spoke, they both heard the sound of cars pulling up in the driveway, the glare of the lights flashing in the window. Lyle instinctively turned toward the movement of the lights, pulling the rifle away from Martin as he looked out the window. Martin did not hesitate, leaping to his feet and sprinting from the room. Behind him he could hear Lyle swear and start after him in pursuit.

There were no lights on in the living room, and Martin stumbled, slamming his shin into a coffee table. He barely kept himself upright, staggering from the table into an armchair with his bad shoulder. Colors spun in his eyes from the wash of pain that swept over him. Still he did not stop moving forward, toward the door. He fumbled with the handle, certain each wasted millisecond would be his last, his vision still not clear, and threw it open, diving out and off the step into the night.

He landed in deep snow, up to his thighs, and lost his balance as he tried to keep going forward, plunging into the drift. Everything was pain. Darkness was everywhere and he could not see. He choked back a desperate sob.

There were shouts behind him, a cacophony of a

hundred voices, none of which he could understand. It spurred him forward, but he stumbled again, wrenching his shoulder in the process. He lost consciousness briefly, slumping into the snowdrift, and came to leaping up as though he were trying to crest above a vast sea.

Shots rang out, echoing through the night. More shouts and cries followed. Martin slumped back into the drift, lying upon it, and closed his eyes, letting the falling snow gather upon his face.

26

Martin awoke the next day to find himself back in his hospital bed. This time he elected to stay where he was and wait for someone to come tell him all that had happened the night before. His stomach ached from a formless anxiety, and he tried to still it by thinking of Lara, counting the days that remained until her return. Perhaps she would rush back when word reached her that he had been injured in the line of duty. That was a foolish thought and he knew it, but he hoped it all the same.

Grenier came to see him later that day, looking as though she had spent most of the night awake.

"How are you doing?" she said, attempting a smile.

Martin shrugged and winced in pain.

"About the same as me, I guess," she said, touching her head. "Hurts like hell."

"I'm just glad you're still walking. How's Malbeck?"

"He got it worse than me. Hargreaves broke his jaw."

Martin made a face. "And Hargreaves?"

"In critical in Medicine Hat. They don't know if he'll make it. Same with that rancher he shot, apparently."

Martin nodded, pushing himself into more of a sitting position. "What about Carol? His wife. Did they find her?"

"Yeah, she was pretty beat up, but all right. She confessed everything. She and Seedstrom were having an affair and wanted to get Hargreaves and that woman out of the picture. When they confronted her, she threatened to expose all his little schemes—apparently there was more than just the stolen gas—if he raised the lease, and he convinced Carol that murder was the best option. They were going to try to pin it on Lyle. Had the gun and some other stuff planted in the house for you to find. If not for the storm..."

"I would have gotten a warrant and found it," Martin finished. Would he have been fooled by the false evidence? He told himself no, that Lyle had no obvious motive, but he had his doubts.

"You did pretty good, handling this on your own," Grenier said. "I couldn't imagine being out here all by myself. It doesn't seem like you can trust what anyone seems or says."

"After this, it sure as hell doesn't," Martin said. "Nobody was what I thought they were. I thought I was doing good work out here before. Now I don't know. Now it just feels like I got lucky."

"People get away from you," she said, and he nodded. "How'd you know Pedersson was involved."

Martin shrugged. "It was a hunch, I guess. I couldn't figure out why he was so nervous to see me when I saw him and Cory at the hotel diner after Cory picked up the body. At first I just though it was because they were involved in the gas thefts. Then it occurred to me that, since Gary couldn't go out to search for the documents himself, because he had to call in the gas theft, he would send his minions. So the reason Russell was having lunch with Cory was because they'd both just gotten back into town."

"Makes sense," Grenier said.

"I got lucky in a guess. There was no way to say for sure that Cory had told Gary he got called out to pick up the body. Why would he, except he's naturally blabby? And they'd stolen the gas the night before, so they would all have called into Gary to see what they should do about the deliveries with the storm."

"I don't if that's luck. I'd say you know quite about these folks and how they operate." Grenier smiled. She left him to rest, heading out of the hospital to rejoin the forensics team that was now combing over the various crime scenes.

Martin was released from the hospital the next day, with strict orders not to return to duty. He did not, letting the forensics team and the Youngstown and Hanna detachments sort through the remaining loose ends. Grenier or someone else would call or stop by and let him know what they had learned, and he received the information with a kind of calm detachment, as though he were hearing a story on the news involving people from some other town.

Cory and Russell both confirmed that Gary had sent Russell in with Cory to try to find the lease documents that Kristi apparently had on her when she was shot. None of them had realized how far down into the coulee the car was, or had known the coulee at all. Russell had abandoned his attempt after an hour and rejoined Cory, who was waiting off the highway just past Wayne's place. Martin had driven past them on his way back into town without even realizing it.

They also said that Gary had told them he and Kristi were working together to get rid of Carol, implying they were having an affair as well, in the hopes of throwing the police off the scent once the murder happened. It had the added benefit of giving Lyle a clear motive. Finally, they outlined the various thefts they had been part of with Gary at the UFA. In addition to the gas, they had stolen lumber, piping, wire, and all sorts of parts, which Russell or Cory would resell.

Carol told the rest. She had told Lyle that she killed

Kristi in the heat of an argument over the Tea House. Lyle had been suspicious but gone along with it, helping Gary to dump the body and, so he assumed, the gun. But Gary had kept it, giving it to Carol to plant. Lyle began to suspect Carol was up to something, and followed her to the motel where she was meeting with Gary, ostensibly to confirm the missing documents had been found. He caught them in the act and forced Gary into the bathroom, where he killed him.

"She said he was wild after that—something broke in him," Grenier said to Martin. She had stopped by to have an afternoon coffee at his place. Outside the temperature had finally drifted above freezing, and their conversation was punctuated by the steady drip of melting snow coming off his roof.

"He couldn't believe she'd betray him like that, set him up for murder. Just flat out refused to. Not that it stopped him from kicking the shit out of her and tying her up. But he had to save her, so he went looking for the documents. Gary didn't have them, so he assumed they must still be in the car. When they weren't there, he realized Gary had probably got one of his minions to do the dirty work, and went to Russell's."

Martin shook his head, giving her a rueful smile. "I wonder where the damn things went. Did they even exist?"

"You want to know where they were?" Grenier said with a grin. "She threw them in the dumpster out back. Must have been right before she got shot."

Martin wanted to laugh, but he felt bleak as well. One person had been killed, with two others possibly to follow, all over a mistake compounded. Grenier and others brought still more evidence that they unearthed, tying everything together, but he had no heart to hear any more. The whole thing seemed like a cruel joke.

He spent most of the rest of the week in his house, and when he finally emerged it was to spring. The snow was mostly gone and the world smelled of earth and greenery, though none had appeared just yet. It would soon, he knew; the grass would begin to turn and the trees would bud. The world would begin anew after the devastation of winter.

EXCERPT:

STAND BY YOUR MAN

Tammy Fairchild left Loverna to escape her reputation and make a new life in a new town. But problems seem to follow her wherever she goes.

Starting over, she finds herself a new job and a new man, someone she can trust. For Kevin Burscht is not like the other men she's known. He is caring and considerate.

But not everything is as it seems with Kevin. He has a mysterious past filled with dark secrets. And Tammy finds that she is the one who will pay the price for his wrongs...

Following the events of The Devious Kind, Stand By Your Man is a taunt thriller about a young woman who discovers the only person she can trust is herself.

HER PARENTS NAMED HER Tammy after the singer of *Stand By Your Man*, a song which she never had much taste for. Country had never been her thing. In high school she acquired another nickname, "trucker fucker", after a rumor started that she waited outside the hotel bar in Loverna for the truckers to come out so she could give them blowjobs. That was not true, or at least not entirely. There had been one guy she gave head to, but she was fairly certain he worked on a seismic rig.

It hadn't mattered though, the name and the story that went with it had stuck and for the rest of high school she was one of those girls. The girl that every guy thought he should try his luck with at a party, whether or not he had a girlfriend. She played the part a few times, mostly out of spite with the boyfriends of girls who taunted her for her sluttiness. It all backfired predictably, with the blame all coming her way.

After high school, lacking the grades and the money to go off to college, she moved into town off her father's farm and took a job at the UFA gas station out on Highway 41. She decided she was done with school and boys and all the drama and nonsense that went with. Now that she was out of school, not interacting with the same one hundred or so horny, judgmental idiots, the nickname and her tawdry reputation began to seem things of the past. She was treated as an adult, accorded that respect, and she began to get it into her head that she deserved a man not a boy, though she did not quite know what that meant.

It led her into the arms of Gary Seedstrom, the UFA store manager, a married man with two young kids. He told her he would leave his wife, that he loved her, but he was no different than the high school boys who leered at her and looked her up and down, asked for a blow job and called her a slut when she didn't comply. Worse, he was a crook and a murderer and tried to use her as an alibi to cover up all his schemes.

That all ended in disaster when Gary was killed himself. Before that, Tammy had the satisfaction of exposing his lies to his wife. That had proved a fleeting and ultimately hollow victory, for soon after the whole town knew about her and Gary.

The fact she was discovered, bound and naked in Russell Pedersson's bed, the night Gary's killer was caught also became general knowledge. Never mind that Russell had been tortured and she had been threatened, the whole thing was so sordid no one in town could stop talking about it. Walking the streets of Loverna felt like high school all over again.

Tammy left after that, unable to face everyone's stares, the way they seemed to be accusing her of some crime, as though her continued presence implicated her in some way. She was tired of the way conversation would lull when she approached, and of the whispers that were forever behind her. *I know you're talking about me*, she longed to turn around and say, but she never did. The hurt in her mother's eyes had been the worst of all, worse even than her father calling her damned fool.

She went to Medicine Hat, intimidated by the idea of going to a big city like Calgary or Edmonton, and not knowing where else to go. It was a place she had visited often while growing up, so it offered the comfort of familiarity, with enough of the unknown to still be enticing. Most of all she got something like the anonymity that she craved, with no one that she passed on the street knowing or caring who she was.

Her first job was at a bar named Checkers, where she worked as a waitress. The tips were good, especially after she followed one of the other girl's recommendations and bought herself a couple of short skirts that accentuated her legs. It was more than enough to live on.

She made a mistake her second week, sleeping with one of the bar managers in his office at the back. Somehow everyone knew within the space of a day and, unbeknownst to her, the manager had also been sleeping with one of the other waitresses. The other girls all turned against Tammy, giving her looks that she was only too familiar with.

After that she kept to herself on the job, minding her business and being careful not to go home with any of the staff, or even the customers. That did not stop them from trying, but she soon became adept at slipping out of grasps and removing hands from where they were not wanted, all while keeping her smile firmly in place. She learned how to keep her guard up around people, gradually adjusting to the disorientation of being in a place where everyone didn't know each other and where you didn't have conversations with people while going to get the mail or buy groceries.

It was all very strange and she was left feeling lonely. In spite of everything, she found herself missing Loverna. That all changed when she met Kevin Burscht. He was not like the men she had met before. He was different.

Kevin worked in the oilfields, though he was vague on the specifics of what he did. Something about well site reclamation and parts. He didn't talk much about it, which suited Tammy fine. They met at a Tim Horton's, where

Tammy had gone for breakfast late one morning after working till close at Checkers. The line up was long and the service terrible and she fell to talking with the genial young man with a smile that made her go weak in the knees.

He invited her to join him for breakfast and they talked for over an hour, long after they both finished their coffee and bagels. Kevin asked for her number and they arranged to meet for a drink later that week. It all felt so different from the happenstance and calamity of her other relationships, which she now realized had not been real relationships all. This one was.

Kevin traveled a lot for his work, which meant Tammy saw him only a day or two a week, but that was fine by her. She was learning to enjoy the time she spent on her own, after so many years living underfoot at home and in Loverna. It was surprising to realize how suffocating that had been and how freeing this felt. Her, as yet, ill-defined relationship with Kevin felt of a piece with this new life she was constructing.

Jennifer, the one girl at work who still talked with her, told Tammy to watch herself. "Who knows what he's getting up to when he's out there traveling. You can't trust him."

Tammy knew as well as Jennifer what men like Kevin got up to in the small towns they traveled to for work, but she didn't worry about him. She trusted him, for reasons she couldn't put into words. He was different. Maybe it was his attentiveness, the way he listened to what she said and considered it. Most of the men she had known had seemed only to be waiting for her to finish whatever she was saying so they could start taking her shirt off. He wasn't like that.

When they were together, during dinner or after sex, Tammy would go on and on about her future and her dreams, things that she had never shared with anyone. Kevin would listen and encourage her, but he shared little

160

of his own thoughts. Tammy was so caught up in the emotion of actually being able to say these things to someone that she didn't notice. And when she did, she pushed that thought aside, telling herself it was because he was a guy. Men don't like revealing themselves, she told herself.

One night, when he had come over very late, after the initial urgency of passion had left them and they were lying in each other's arms, Tammy mentioned that she wanted to move to Vancouver.

"Why?" Kevin said, his voice dim, as if he were already starting to drift off to sleep.

"I don't know. I've never seen the ocean before. I'd love to see it. And it just seems so cool. There's so much happening there."

"Mmm," Kevin said.

Tammy looked over and could see his eyes were half-closed. "What about you? Where do you want to live?"

"Not Vancouver."

"Why not?"

"I'm from there," Kevin said, a pained frown crossing his face and then vanishing.

"Really," Tammy said. "And you wouldn't go back?"

There was a long pause, during which she wondered if he was asleep, before Kevin replied. "I can't."

"Why not?" Tammy asked, but received no reply as Kevin's breathing deepened and slowed.

"What do you think he means?" Tammy asked Jennifer when they were next on shift together.

"Nothing good."

Jennifer was only a year or two older than Tammy, and with her sleight frame she looked even younger, but she seemed to have decades more experience, at least to the girl from Loverna. She had, it seemed, dated every kind of bad man—and every man was bad in some kind of way, according to her. That was a fact as inescapable as gravity.

Everything about Kevin was a mark of suspicion for her. His absences for work, his refusal to share much about his feelings or his life. All of it was proof that he was no good.

"You only can't go back to a place if you've done something wrong. Vancouver's a big place. If he's worried about being found there, it must be something really wrong."

Jennifer had a way of speaking that gave her an authority. She sounded like she knew what she was talking about. And yet Tammy wasn't sure.

Nothing more came of the conversation, no matter how Tammy tried to pry and steer Kevin in that direction. He seemed oblivious to her attempts and wouldn't say anything more on the matter. Not when she brought up his parents, or high school, or his friends. It was as if that part of him had ceased to exist once he left British Columbia.

Tammy told herself not to let it bother her. There could be a lot of reasons for that, after all. Not everyone had happy childhoods they wished to return to, as she well knew.

She did not dwell on the matter. For all his reticence and his frequent absences, he was the most present of the men she had been with. After three months she contemplated telling him she loved him, but her courage failed her. It seemed perilous to risk upsetting something that was so precious to her and seemed so perfect. For she knew nothing this good could last forever.

ABOUT THE AUTHOR

Clint Westgard is an author of mystery and crime thrillers, as well as science fiction and fantasy novels. These include the epic fantasy The Shadow Men and the science fiction epic The Sojourners Cycle. In addition, he has published a work of historical fantasy set in colonial Peru, The Maleficio Chronicles, and a retelling of the Minotaur legend, The Trials of the Minotaur. Clint Westgard lives in Calgary, Alberta.

ALSO BY CLINT WESTGARD

The Maleficio Chronicles

Luisa is always more than she appears. Rumor and mystery surround her. And strange events seem to follow wherever she goes.

Born in Lima, City of Kings, to a noble family, her father so fears her true nature that he banishes her to a convent. There she falls under the suspicion of the Inquisition and decides to flee.

Disguised as a man, she embarks upon a series of wild adventures, dueling, carousing, and gambling her way across colonial Peru. But everything changes when someone recognizes her for what she truly is, and soon she finds herself fighting for her very survival.

In a world where she will always stand apart, Luisa undergoes a strange journey, marked by betrayal and murder, terrible powers and mysterious strangers. *The Maleficio Chronicles* is her incredible confession and a story like no other.

ALSO BY CLINT WESTGARD

Realm of Shadows
Volume One of The Shadow Men

Craitol and Renuih, two empires a world apart, divided by
the desert that lies between them. A desert ruled by the
Shadow Men.

An uneasy peace holds sway in both realms, hiding
longstanding feuds and bitter rivalries. Until a Shadow
Men raid on Renuih shatters the calm and sets in motion
events no one can control.

Masiph id Ezern, unfavored son of the Imperial Vazeir,
finds himself a hero following the raid. His father remains
unmoved by his exploits and, in his bitterness, Masiph will
find himself a reluctant participant in a plot against the
empire.

As he finds himself drawn deeper and deeper into the
conspiracy, he soon realizes there will be no escaping the
realm of shadows, where intrigue and betrayal abound.
And though the Shadow Men have gone quiet, they will
not stay silent forever…

ALSO BY CLINT WESTGARD

Council of Shadows
Volume Two of The Shadow Men

Discontent continues to fester within the realms of Craitol
and Renuih, fed by intrigues carried out in the shadows. As
rivals and apostates struggle for supremacy, a long
incubated plan begins to unfold.

Vyissan, a mysterious alkemycal practitioner arrives in
Renuih, the latest strike in a long war over who shall
control the secrets of alkemya and Craitol itself. He carries
with him a secret that, once revealed, will reverberate
across all realms. Before he can reveal it though, the
conspirators against the emperor will strike their own
blow.

But now, a new and more powerful menace looms on the
horizon. The Shadow Men have gained the secrets of the
Council Adept's alkemya and no one can be certain what
they will do with it…

ALSO BY CLINT WESTGARD

Dance of Shadows
Volume Three of The Shadow Men

War with the Shadow Men looms in both realms as the consequences of the Gvers' Council in Craitol begin to make themselves known. A war that could end in glorious triumph or bitter disaster.

Doubt shadows everyone's steps, for they know there are no certainties in the desert. Especially now the Shadow Men have made the art of alkemya their own.

No one has more questions than Vyissan, for he is working in service to a cause he is no longer sure he believes in. And now he must undertake a journey with those who both loathe and fear him. Before the first sword is drawn, his life will be under threat.

But his will not be the only one, for somewhere in the desert the Shadow Men lie in wait…

ALSO BY CLINT WESTGARD

The Forgotten
Volume One of The Sojourners Cycle

Who is David Aeida? And what does he know that has so
many people pursuing him?

David doesn't know. He can't remember anything about
who he is. But he finds himself ensnared in a vicious
conflict between a religious cult and a guild that patrols the
crossings between multiple universes. They will both stop
at nothing to gain whatever knowledge he possesses. Most
dangerous of all, is the implacable hunter, known only as
the Seeker, who has his own reasons for wanting to find
David.

His only hope is to recover his memories before they do.
His only ally is a woman named Meredith, and she
definitely knows more than she is telling…

Spanning both universes and the human mind, The
Forgotten is an unforgettable science fiction thriller that
questions the very nature of identity. It is the first volume
of the Sojourners Cycle, an epic that will encompass the
fates of universes and humanity itself.

ALSO BY CLINT WESTGARD

The Apostate
Volume Two of The Sojourners Cycle

Laila has only one goal in mind. To have her revenge upon the Grand Regent for all he has done to her. First, though, she needs to find her way across the universes.

That is easier said than done. The Grand Regent's agents are still pursuing her. As is the Society of Travellers. And the Seeker lurks somewhere, waiting for his moment to strike.

Laila has a plan, though, and a few tricks of her own. But she will discover that not everything is at seems. For the war she has given her life to hides a far greater conflict.

Spanning multiple universes and the complexities of the human mind, The Apostate, continues the incredible journey begun in The Forgotten. The second volume of The Sojourners Cycle is an unforgettable science fiction epic that encompasses the fates of universes and humanity itself.